H. G. WELLS'S
THE TIME MACHINE

RETOLD BY TERRY DAVIS

ILLUSTRATED BY JOSÉ ALFONSO OCAMPO RUIZ

LIBRARIAN REVIEWER
Katharine Kan
Graphic novel reviewer and Library Consultant, Panama City, FL
MLS in Library and Information Studies, University of Hawaii at Manoa, HI

READING CONSULTANT
Elizabeth Stedem
Educator/Consultant, Colorado Springs, CO
MA in Elementary Education, University of Denver, CO

STONE ARCH BOOKS
MINNEAPOLIS   SAN DIEGO

Graphic Revolve is published by Stone Arch Books,
151 Good Counsel Drive, P.O. Box 669,
Mankato, Minnesota 56002.
www.stonearchbooks.com

Library of Congress Cataloging-in-Publication Data
Davis, Terry.
The Time Machine / H. G. Wells; retold by Terry Davis; illustrated by José Alfonso Ocampo Ruiz.
p. cm. — (Graphic Revolve)
ISBN-13: 978-1-59889-833-0 (library binding)
ISBN-10: 1-59889-833-7 (library binding)
ISBN-13: 978-1-59889-889-7 (paperback)
ISBN-10: 1-59889-889-2 (paperback)
1. Graphic novels. I. Ocampo Ruiz, José Alfonso. II. Wells, H. G. (Herbert George), 1866–1946. Time machine. III. Title.
PN6727.D36T56 2008
741.5'973—dc22 2007006201

Summary: A scientist invents a machine that carries him into the future. While there, he meets a race of gentle humans — and evil underground creatures. Even worse, his time machine, his only chance to escape, is trapped deep inside the Morlock caverns.

Art Director: Heather Kindseth
Graphic Designer: Kay Fraser

1 2 3 4 5 6 12 11 10 09 08 07

Printed in the United States of America

TABLE OF CONTENTS

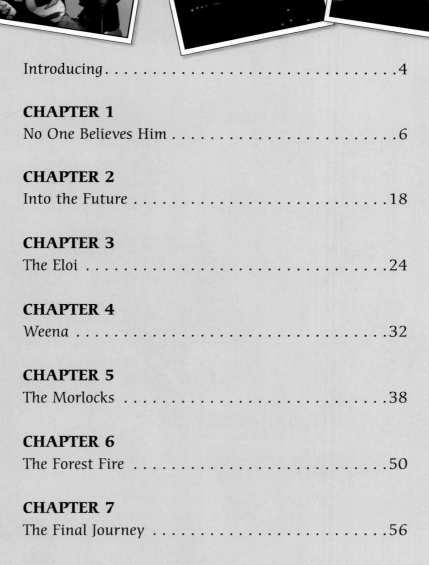

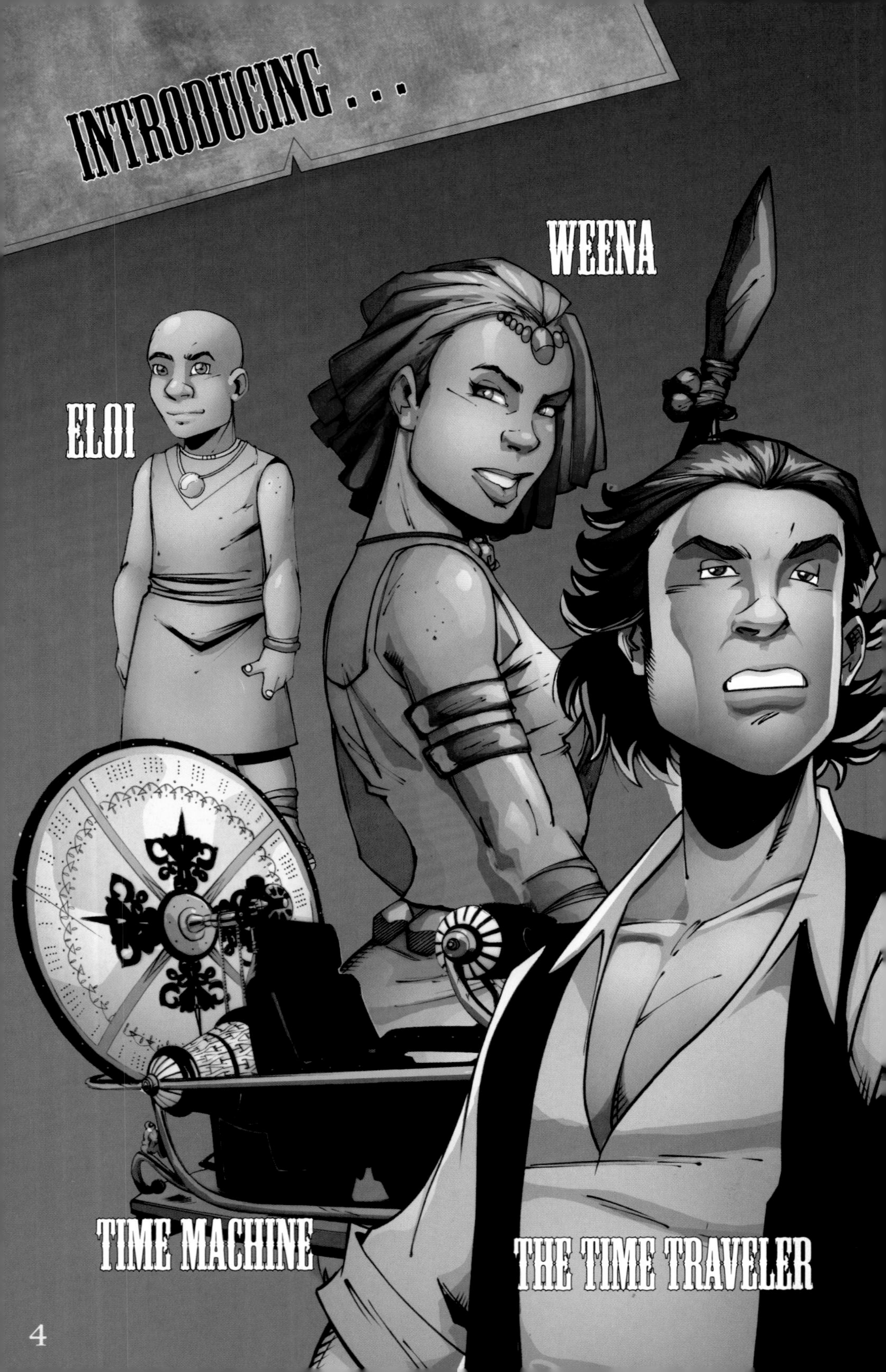
INTRODUCING . . .
WEENA
ELOI
TIME MACHINE
THE TIME TRAVELER

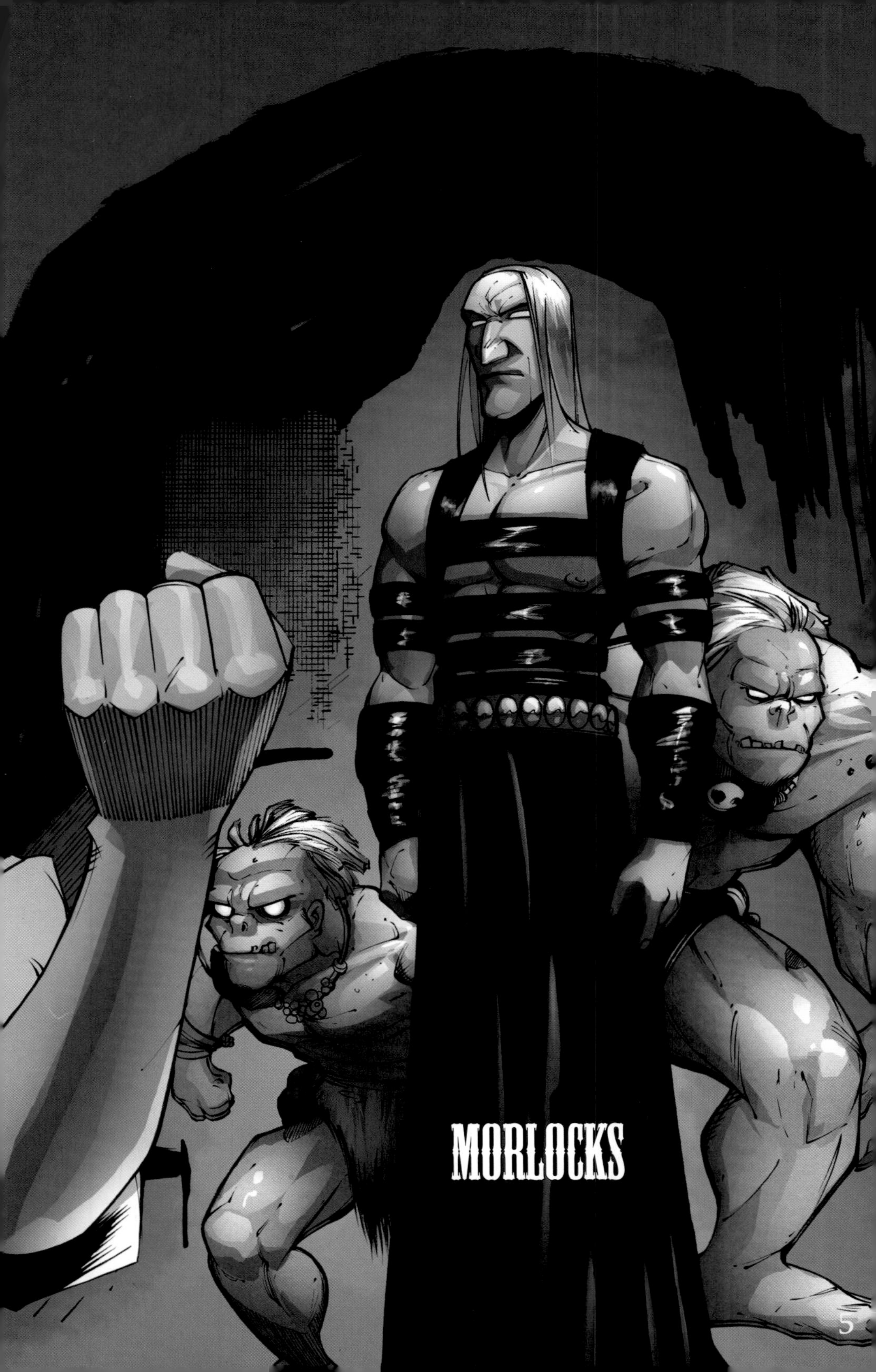
MORLOCKS

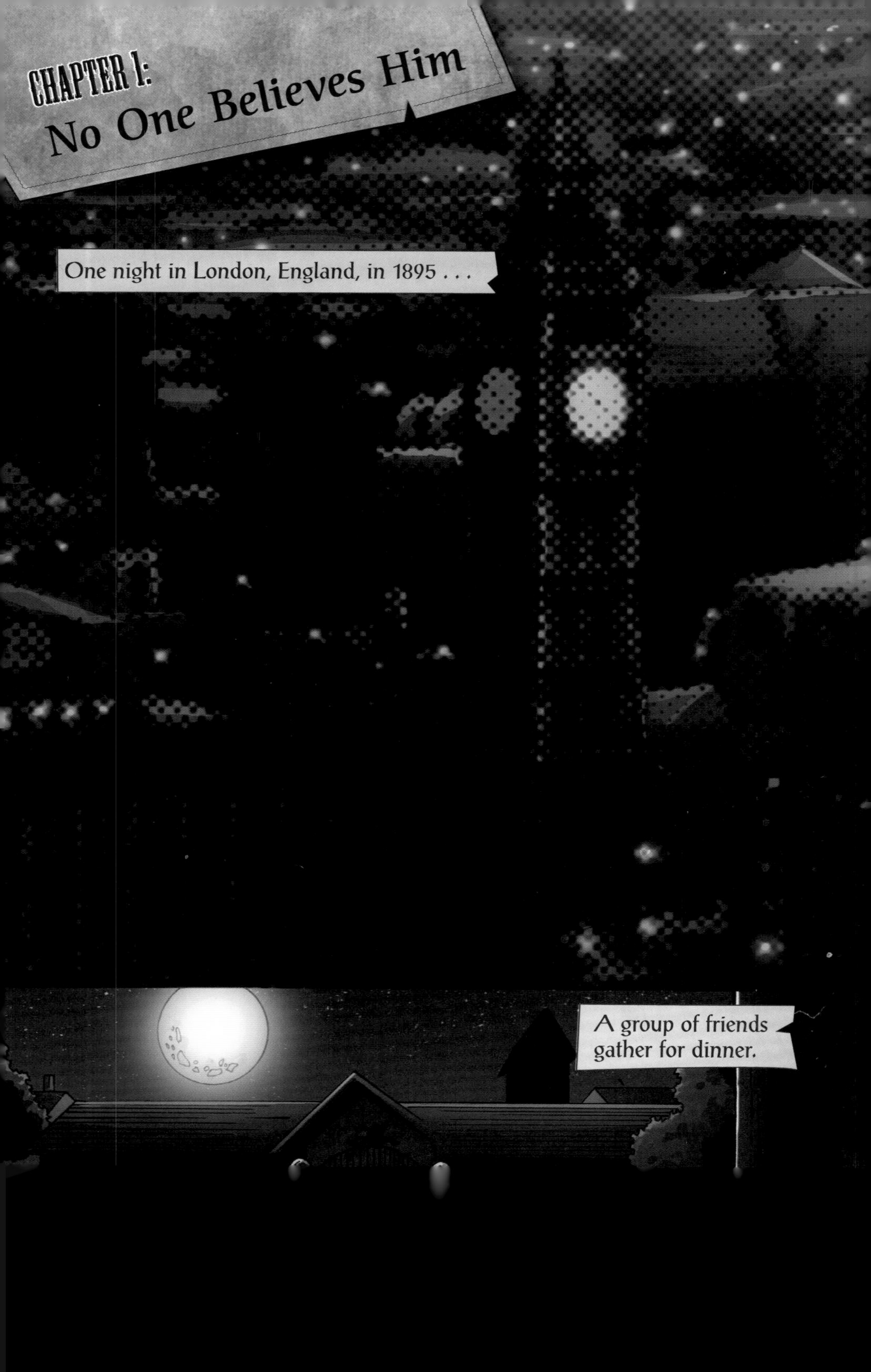
CHAPTER 1:
No One Believes Him
One night in London, England, in 1895 . . .
A group of friends gather for dinner.

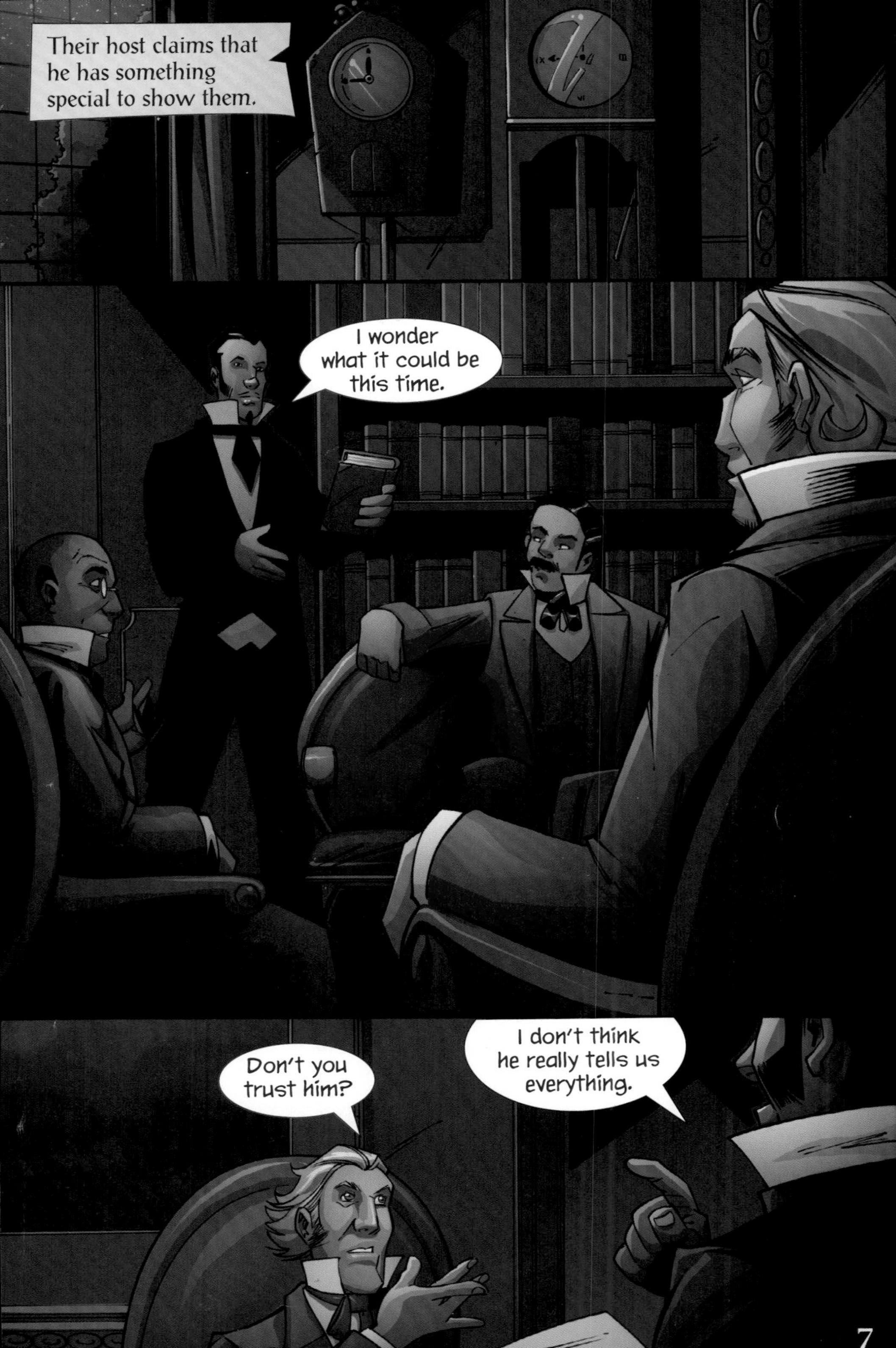
Their host claims that he has something special to show them.
I wonder what it could be this time.
Don't you trust him?
I don't think he really tells us everything.

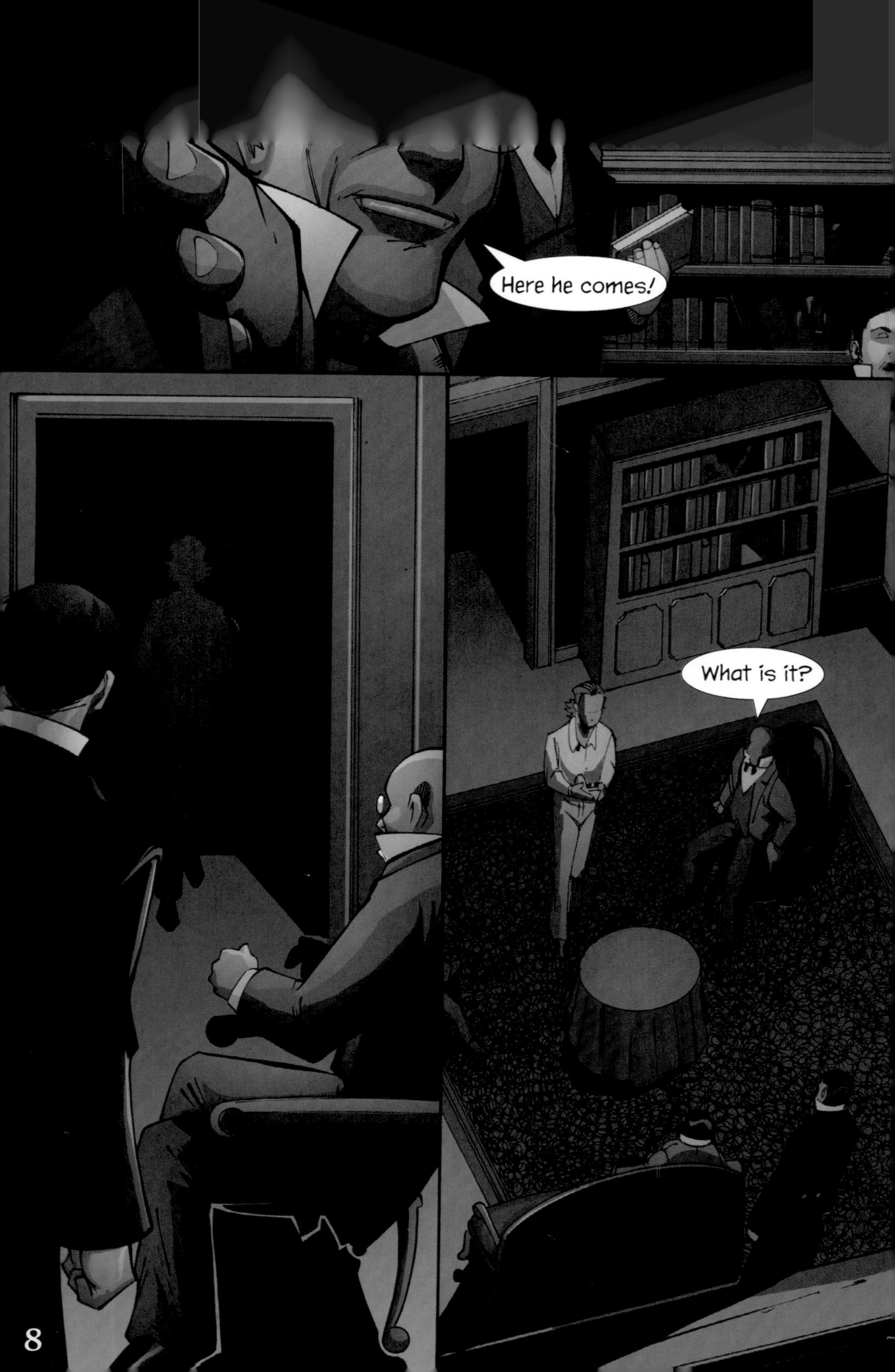
Here he comes!
What is it?

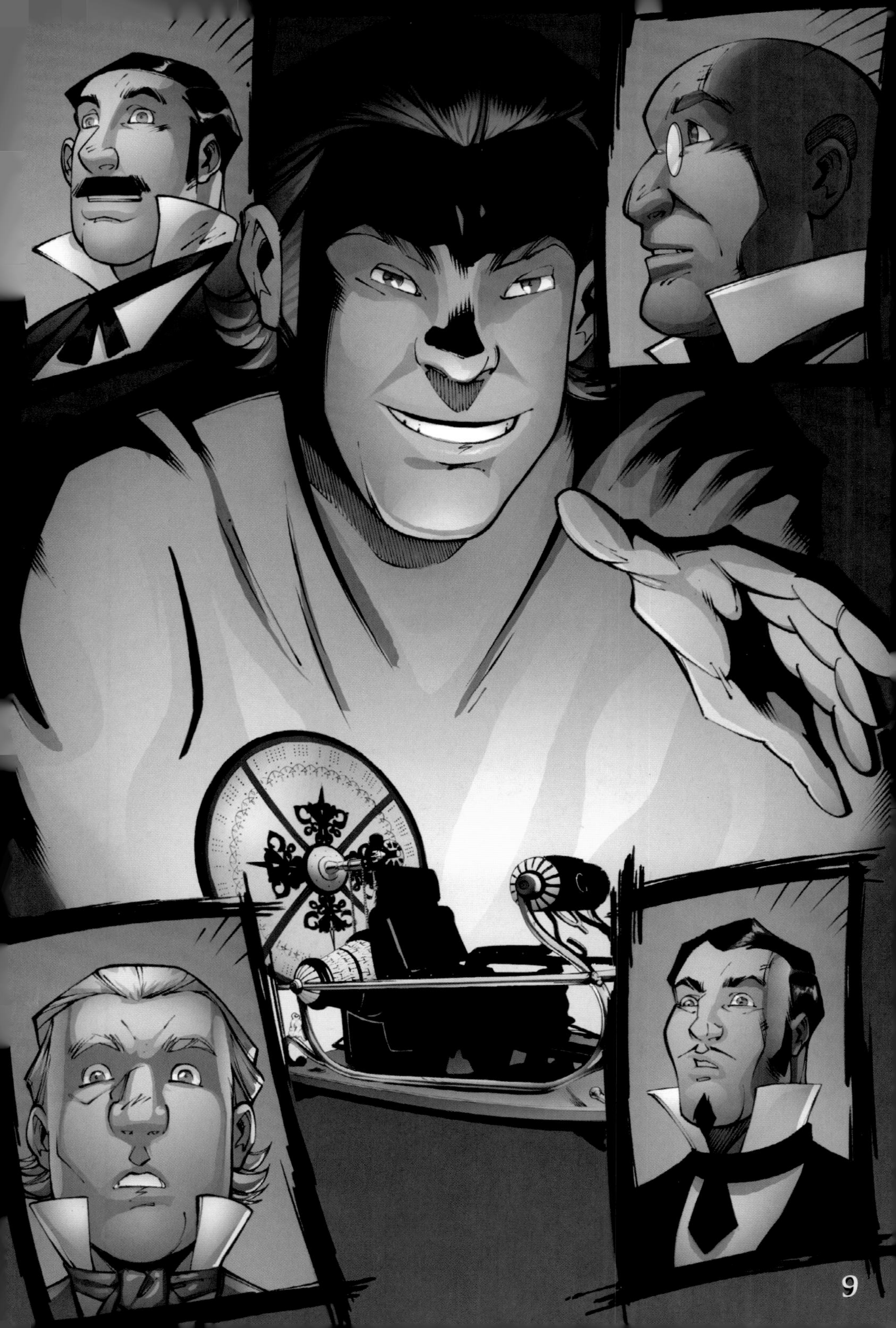

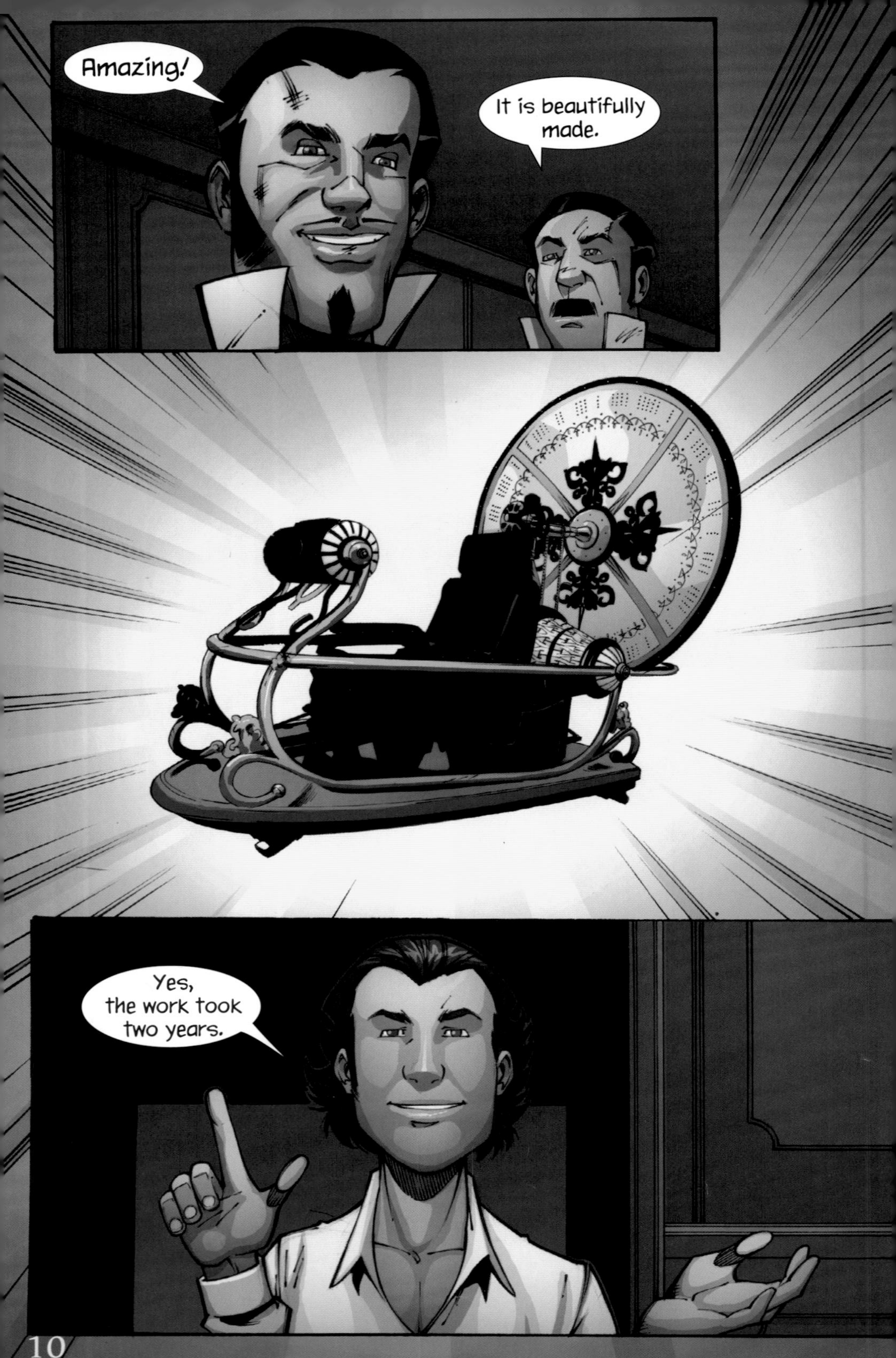
Amazing!
It is beautifully made.
Yes, the work took two years.

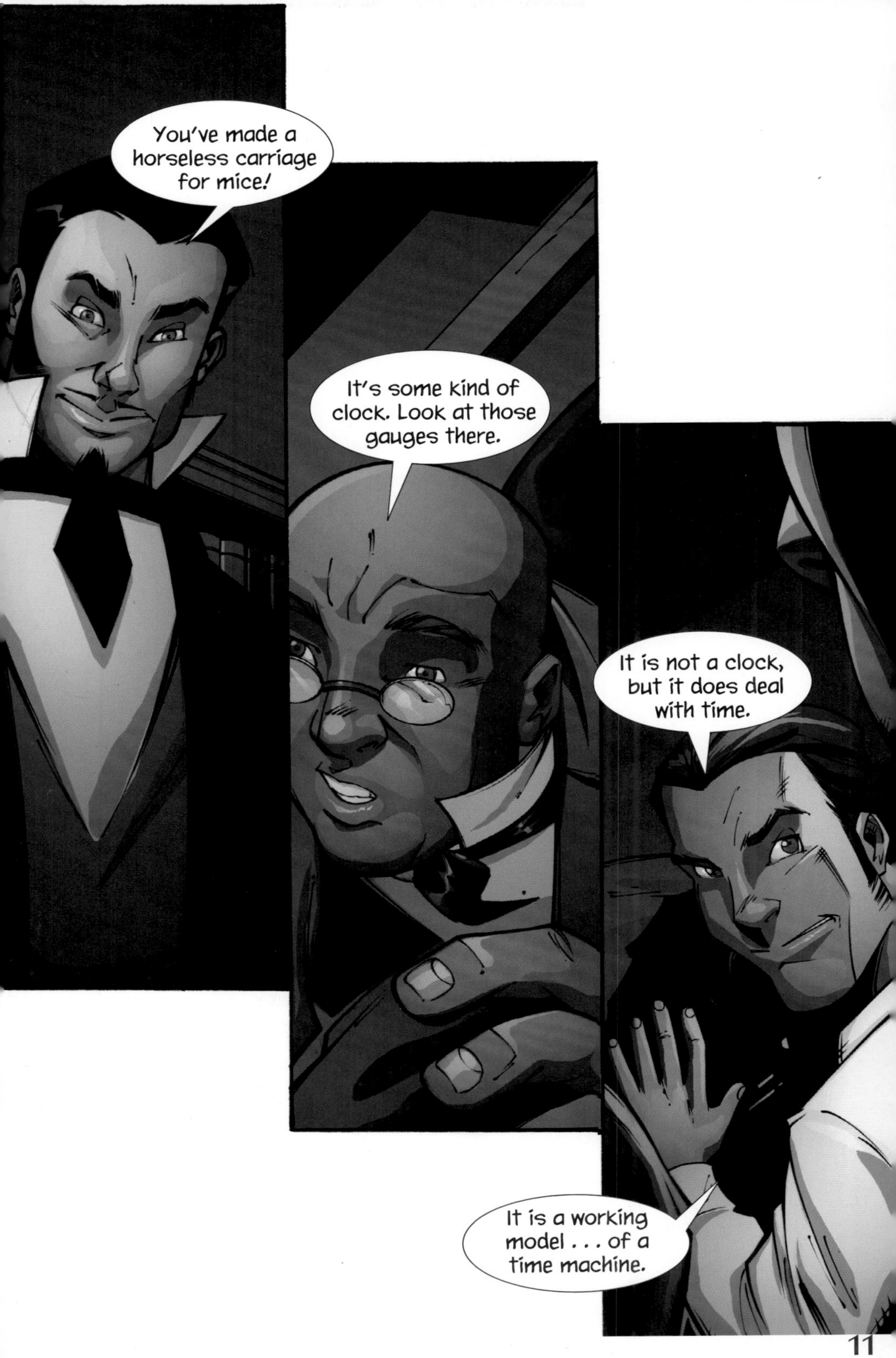
You've made a horseless carriage for mice!
It's some kind of clock. Look at those gauges there.
It is not a clock, but it does deal with time.
It is a working model . . . of a time machine.

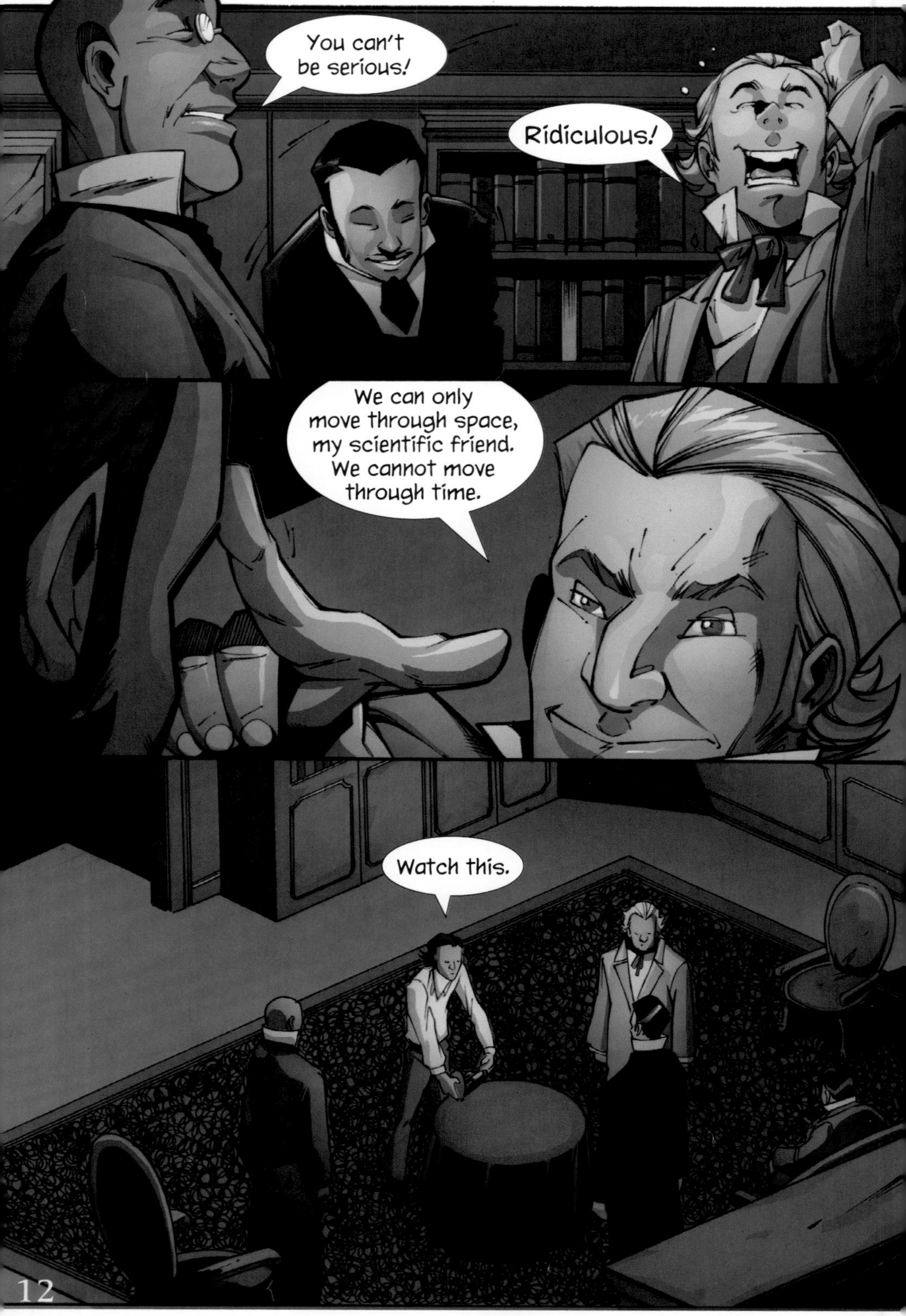
You can't be serious!
Ridiculous!
We can only move through space, my scientific friend. We cannot move through time.
Watch this.

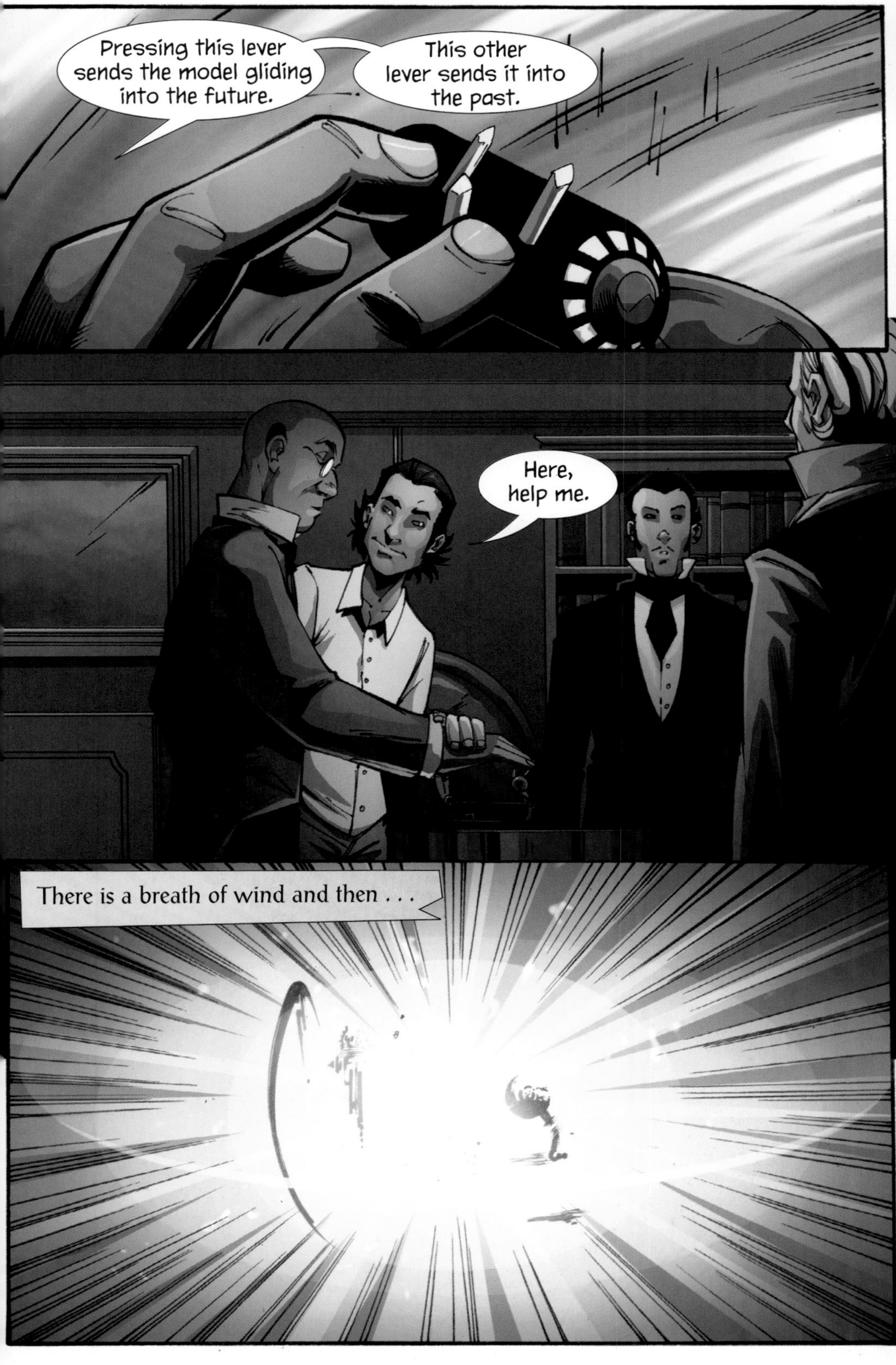

Pressing this lever sends the model gliding into the future.
This other lever sends it into the past.
Here, help me.
There is a breath of wind and then . . .

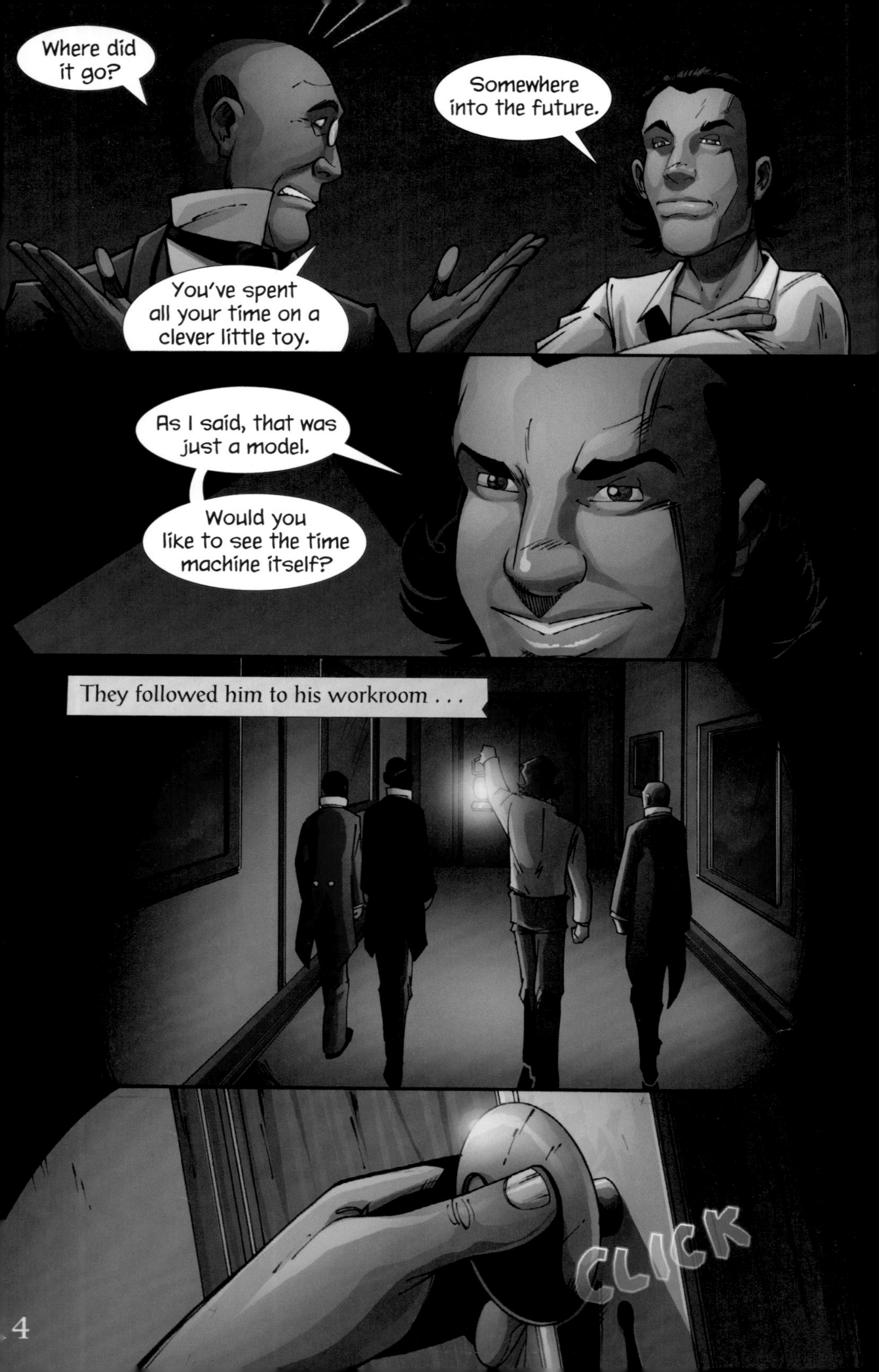
Where did it go?
Somewhere into the future.
You've spent all your time on a clever little toy.
As I said, that was just a model.
Would you like to see the time machine itself?
They followed him to his workroom . . .
CLICK

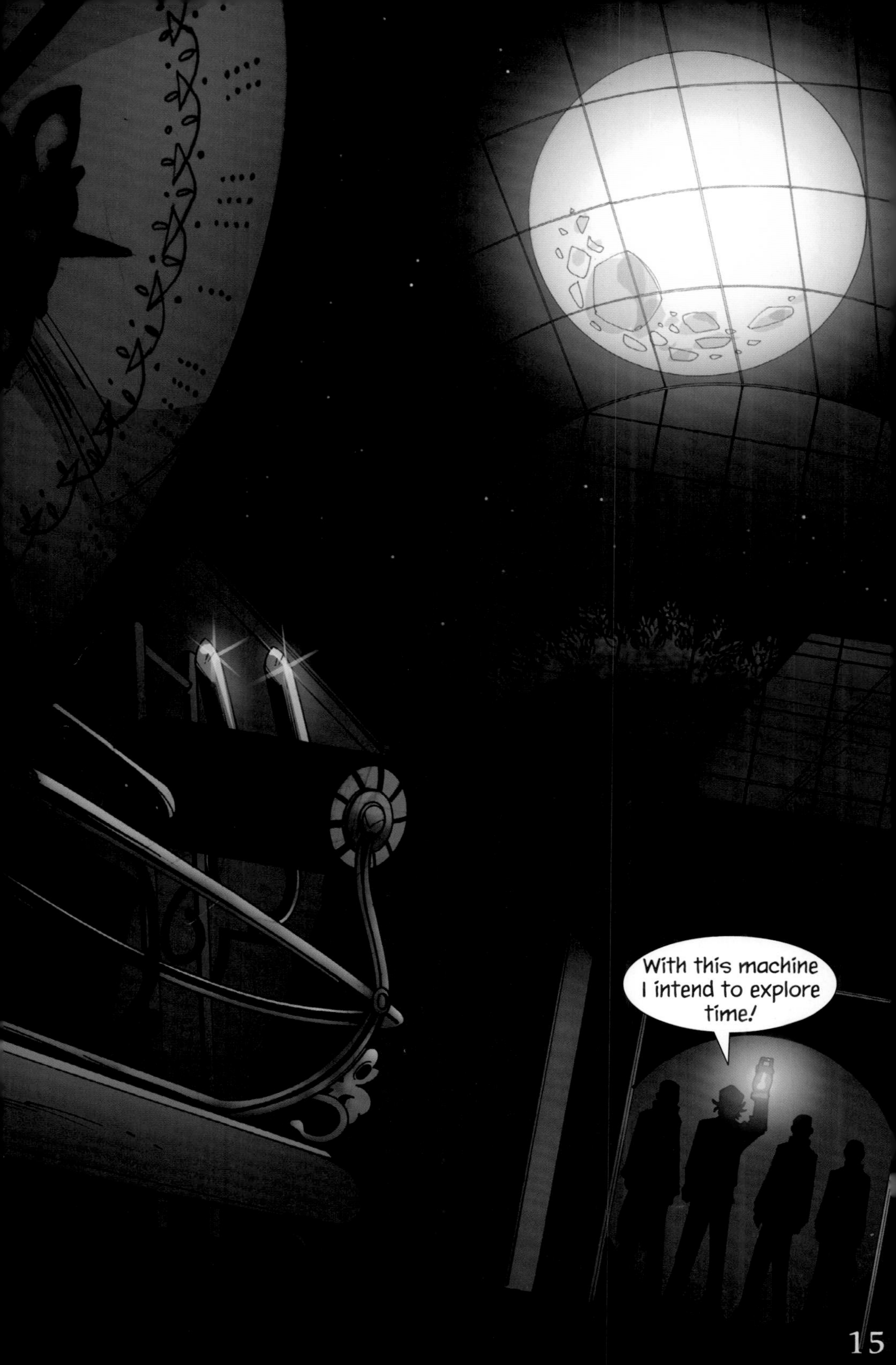
With this machine I intend to explore time!

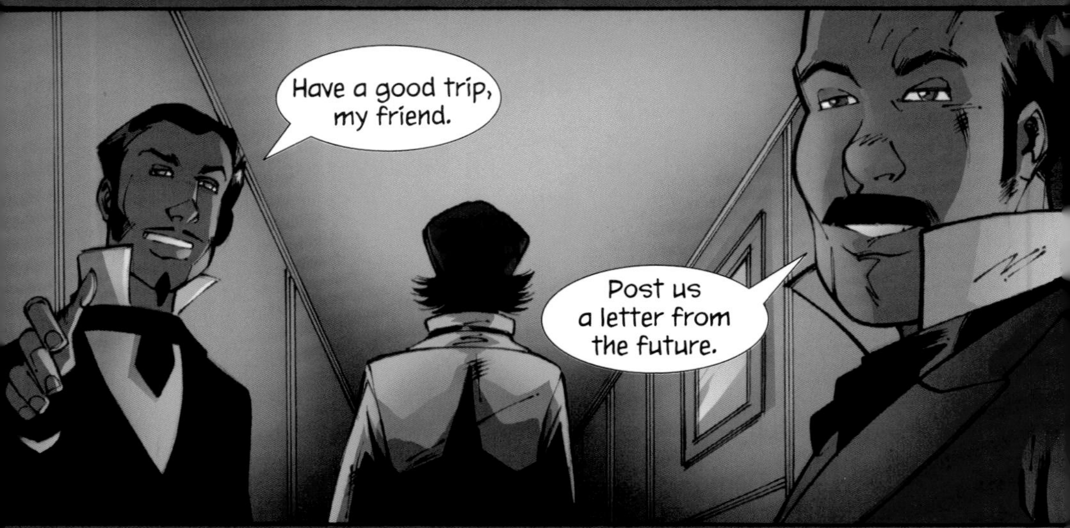
Have a good trip, my friend.
Post us a letter from the future.

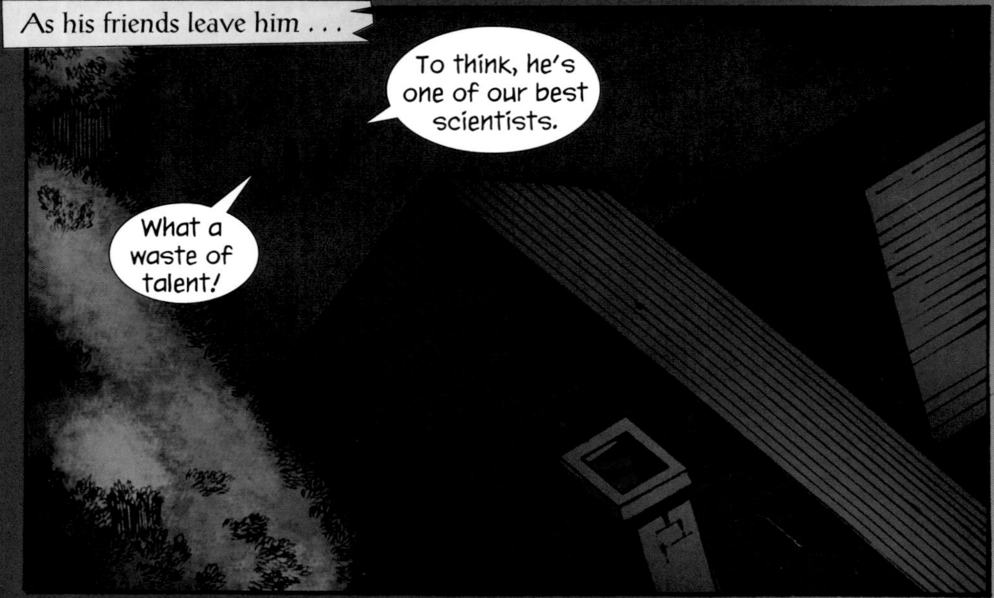
As his friends leave him . . .
To think, he's one of our best scientists.
What a waste of talent!

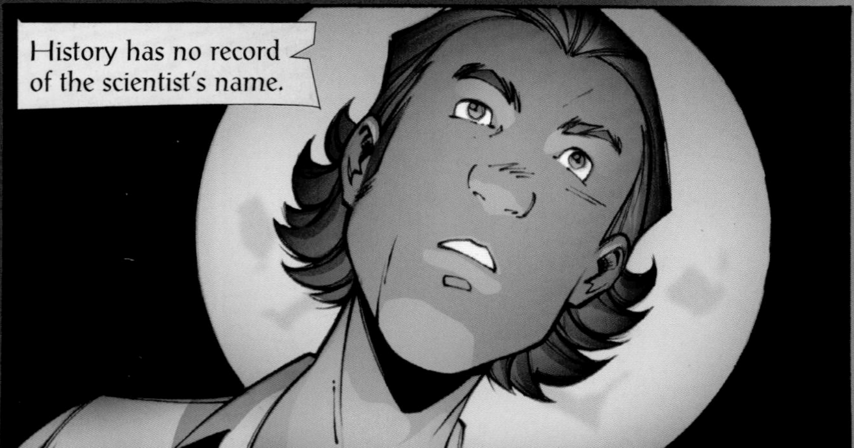
History has no record of the scientist's name.

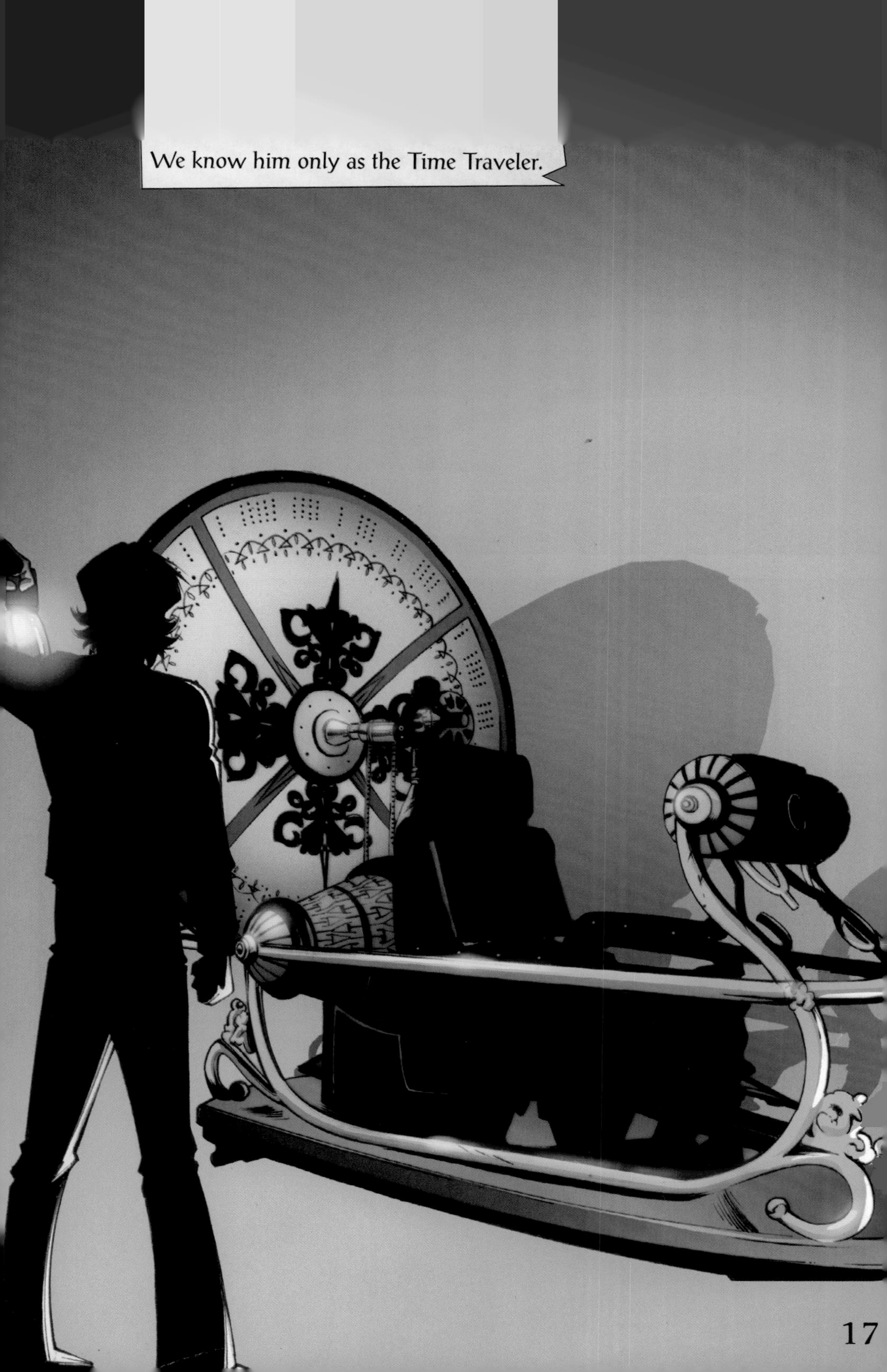
We know him only as the Time Traveler.

CHAPTER 2: Into the Future

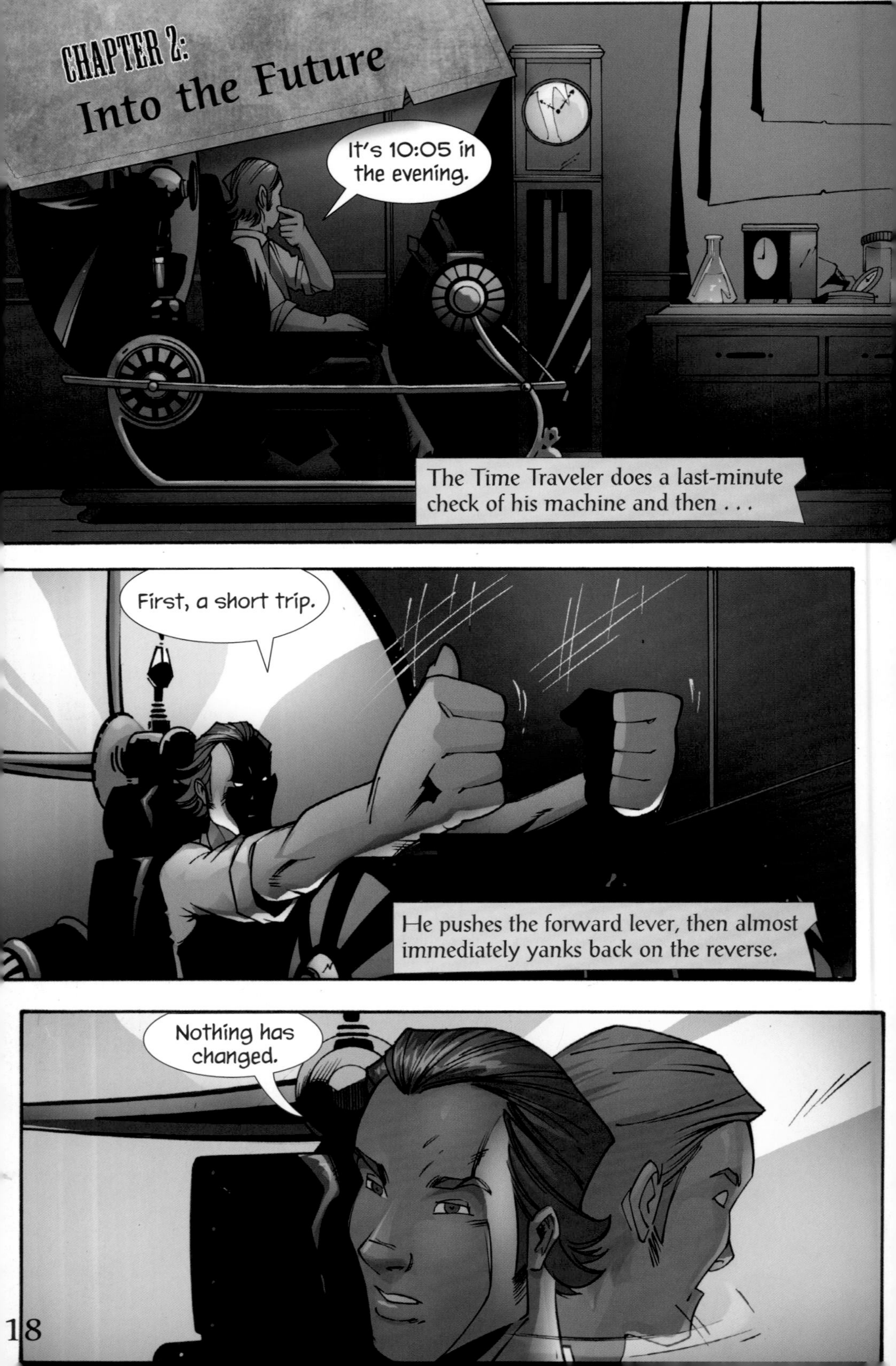
It's 10:05 in the evening.
The Time Traveler does a last-minute check of his machine and then . . .
First, a short trip.
He pushes the forward lever, then almost immediately yanks back on the reverse.
Nothing has changed.

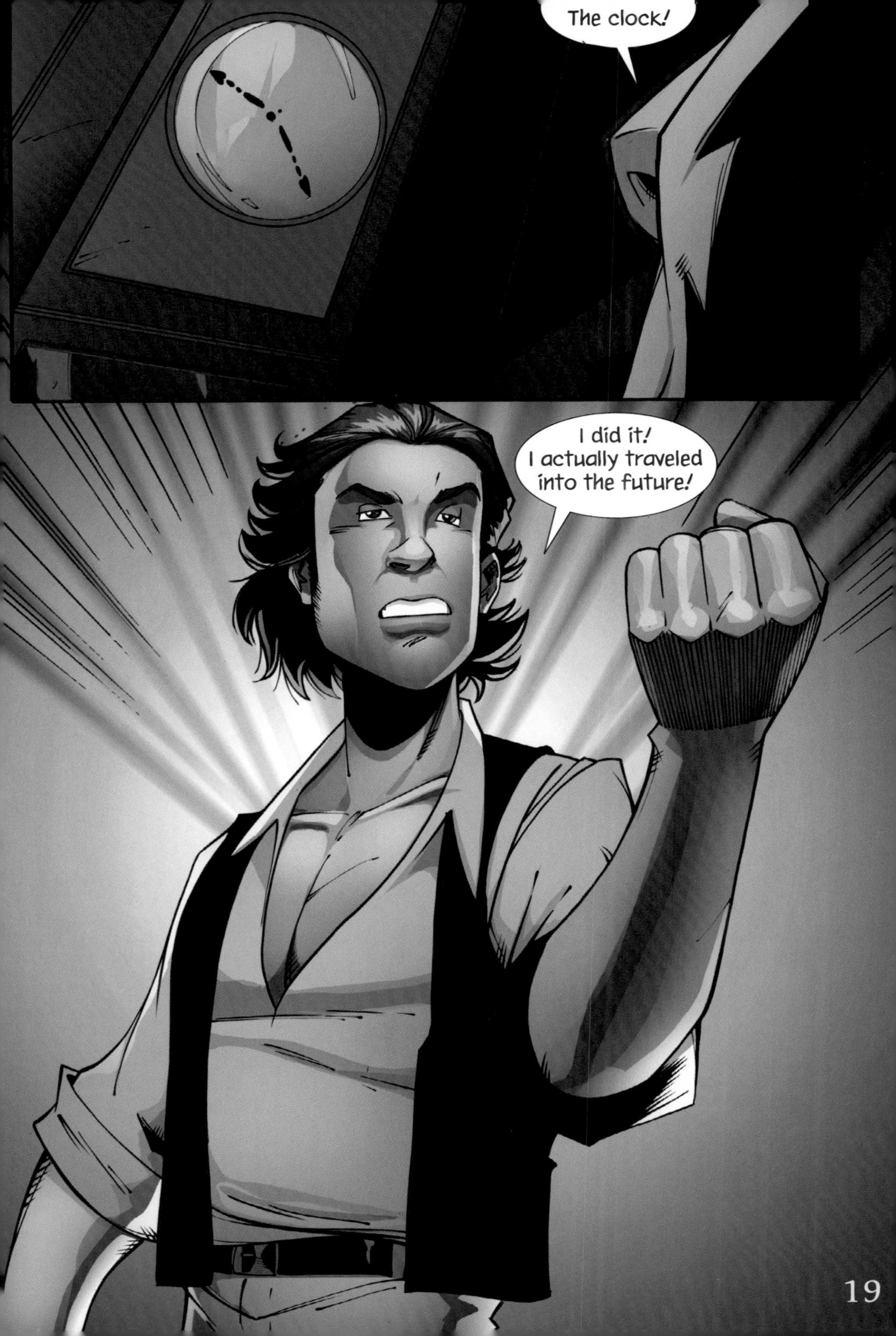
The clock!
I did it! I actually traveled into the future!

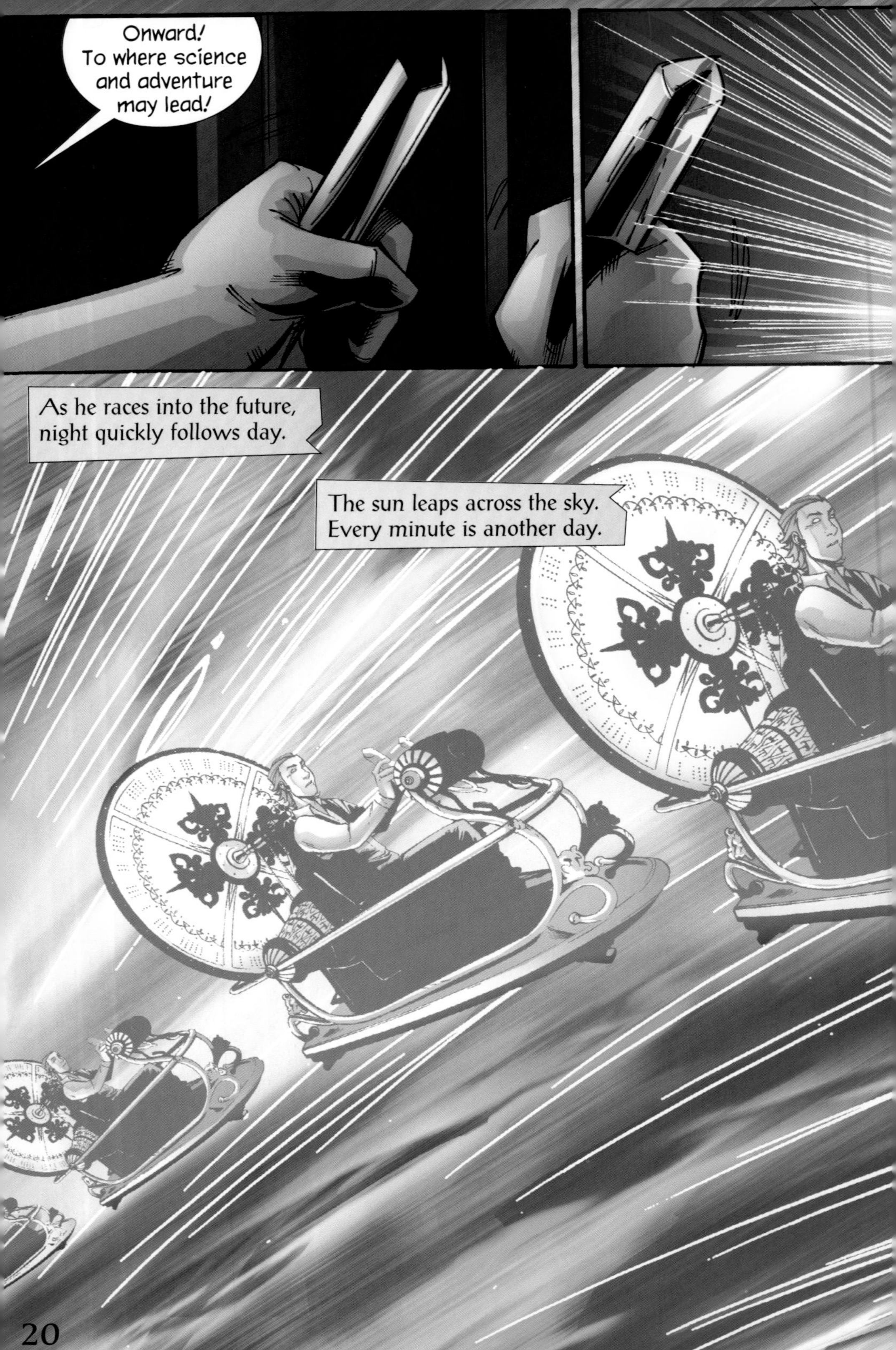
Onward! To where science and adventure may lead!
As he races into the future, night quickly follows day.
The sun leaps across the sky. Every minute is another day.

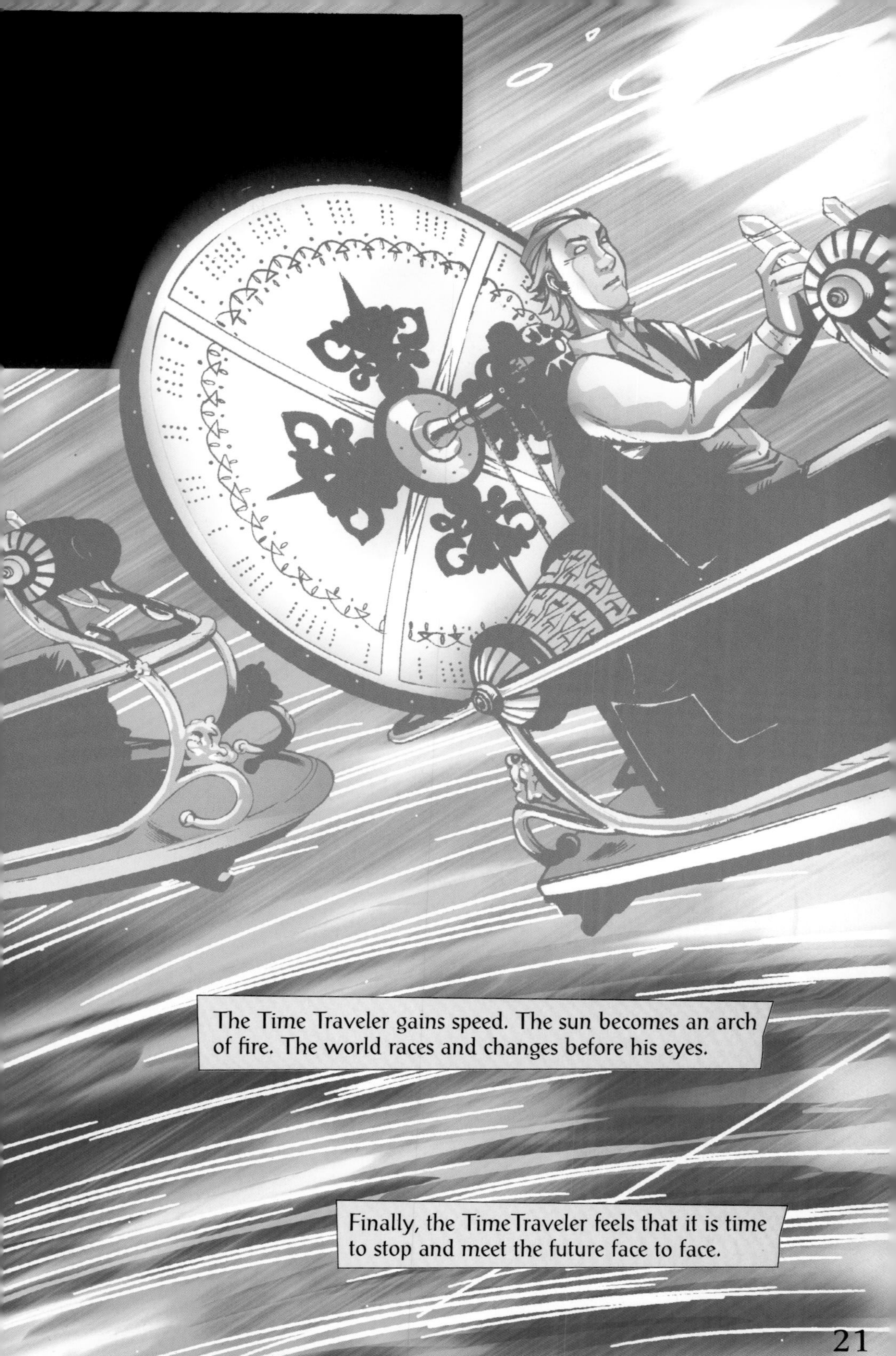

The Time Traveler gains speed. The sun becomes an arch of fire. The world races and changes before his eyes.
Finally, the TimeTraveler feels that it is time to stop and meet the future face to face.

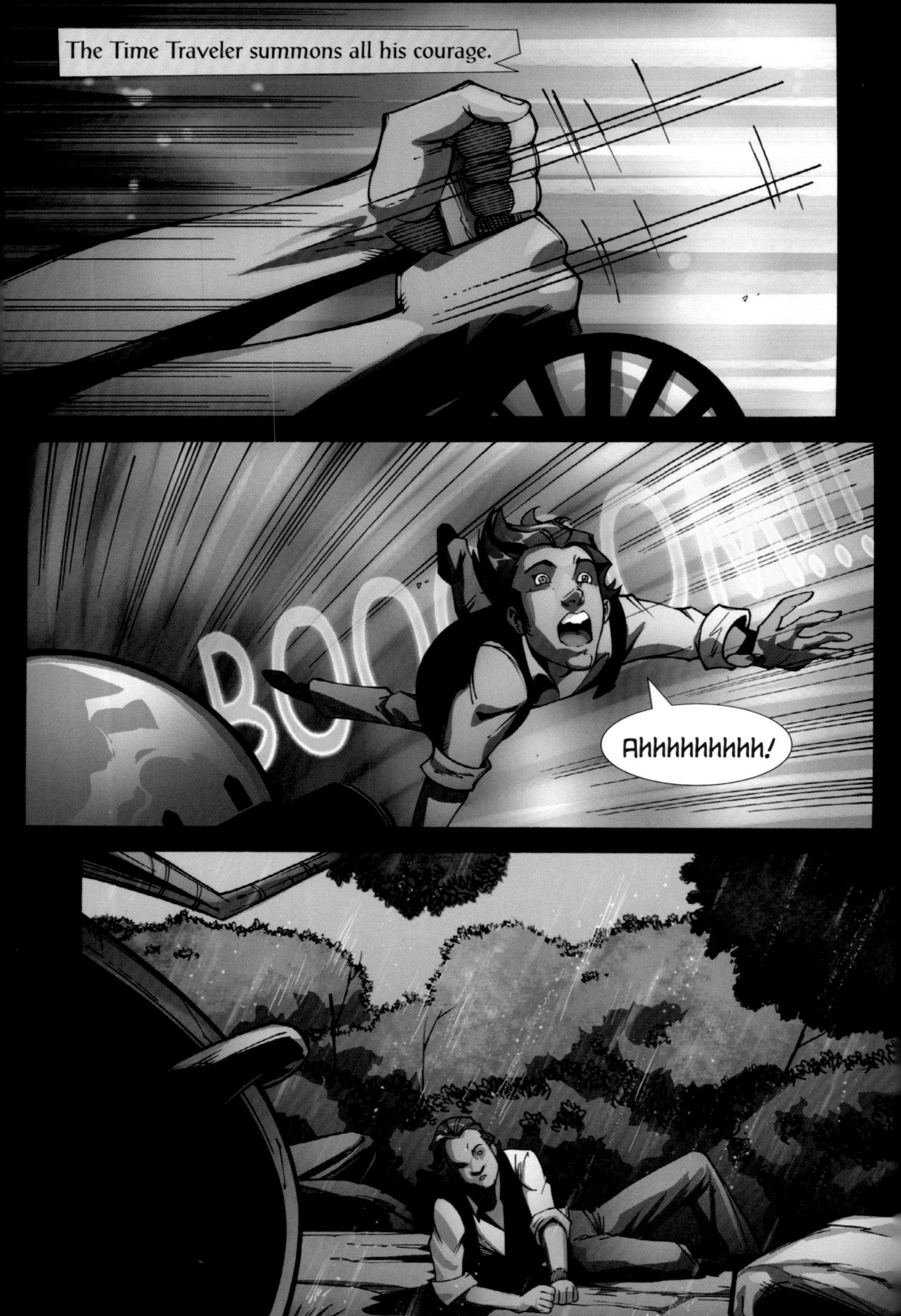
The Time Traveler summons all his courage.
Ahhhhhhhhh!

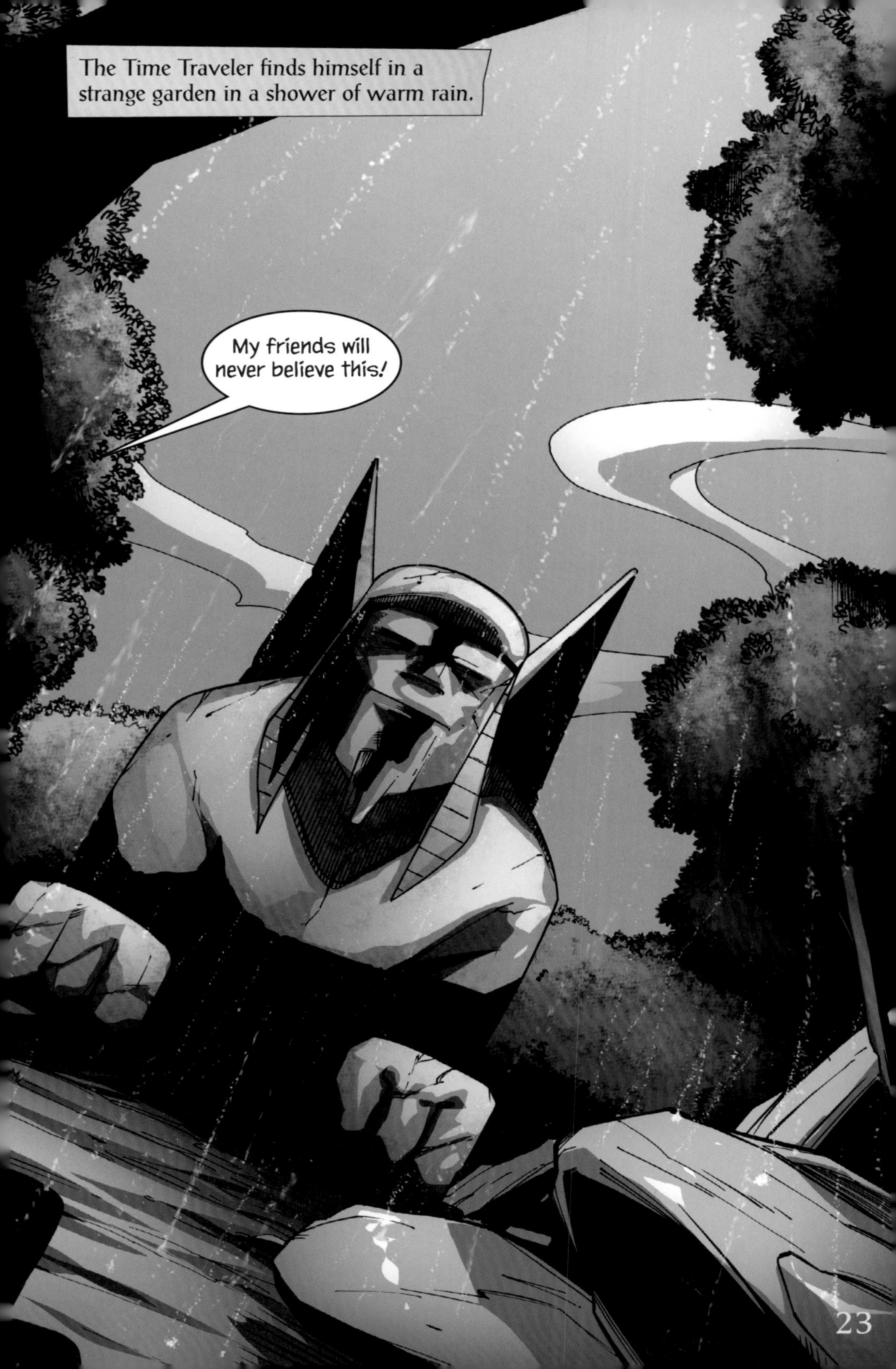
The Time Traveler finds himself in a strange garden in a shower of warm rain.
My friends will never believe this!

CHAPTER 3: The Eloi

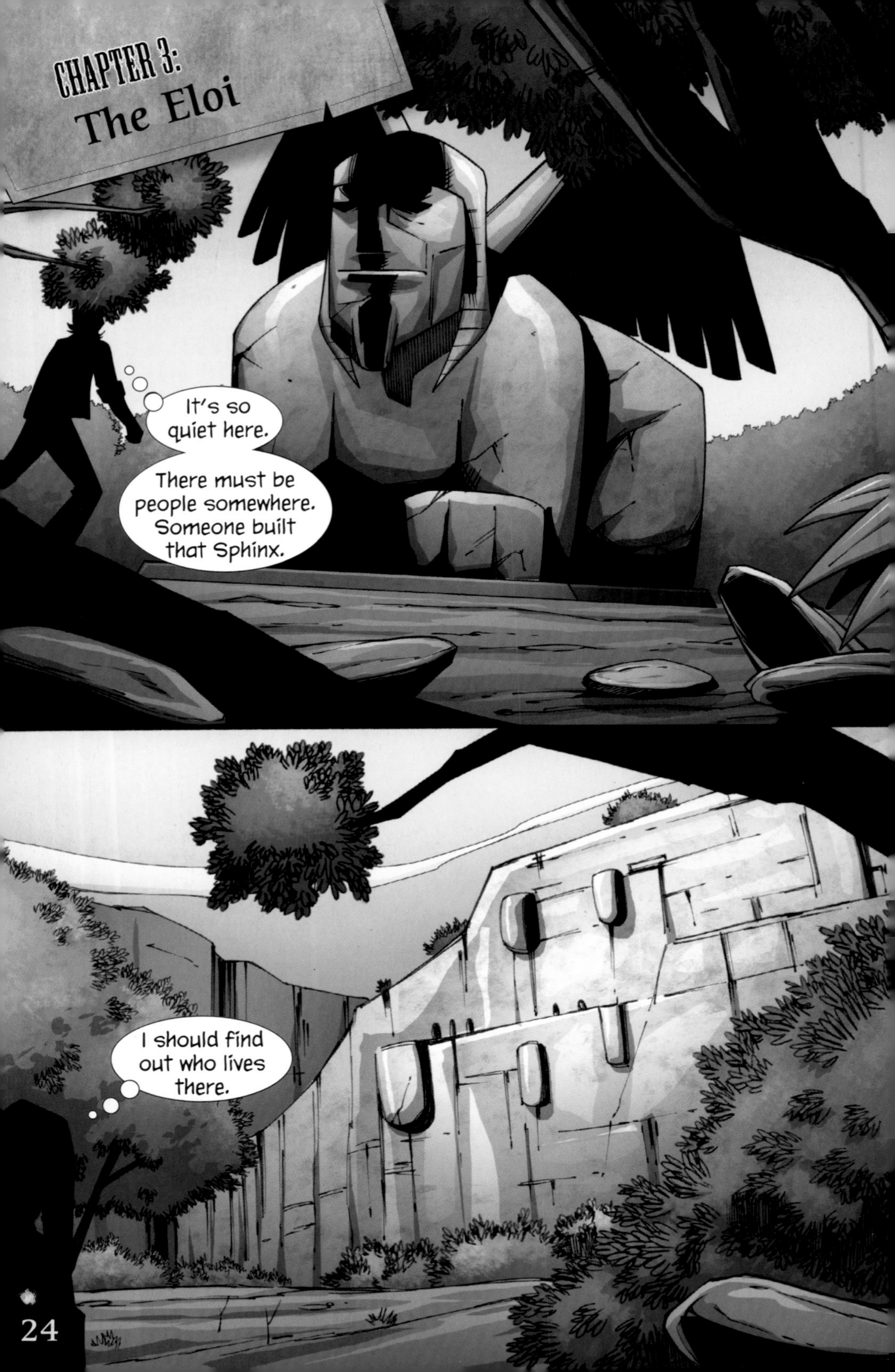
It's so quiet here.
There must be people somewhere. Someone built that Sphinx.
I should find out who lives there.

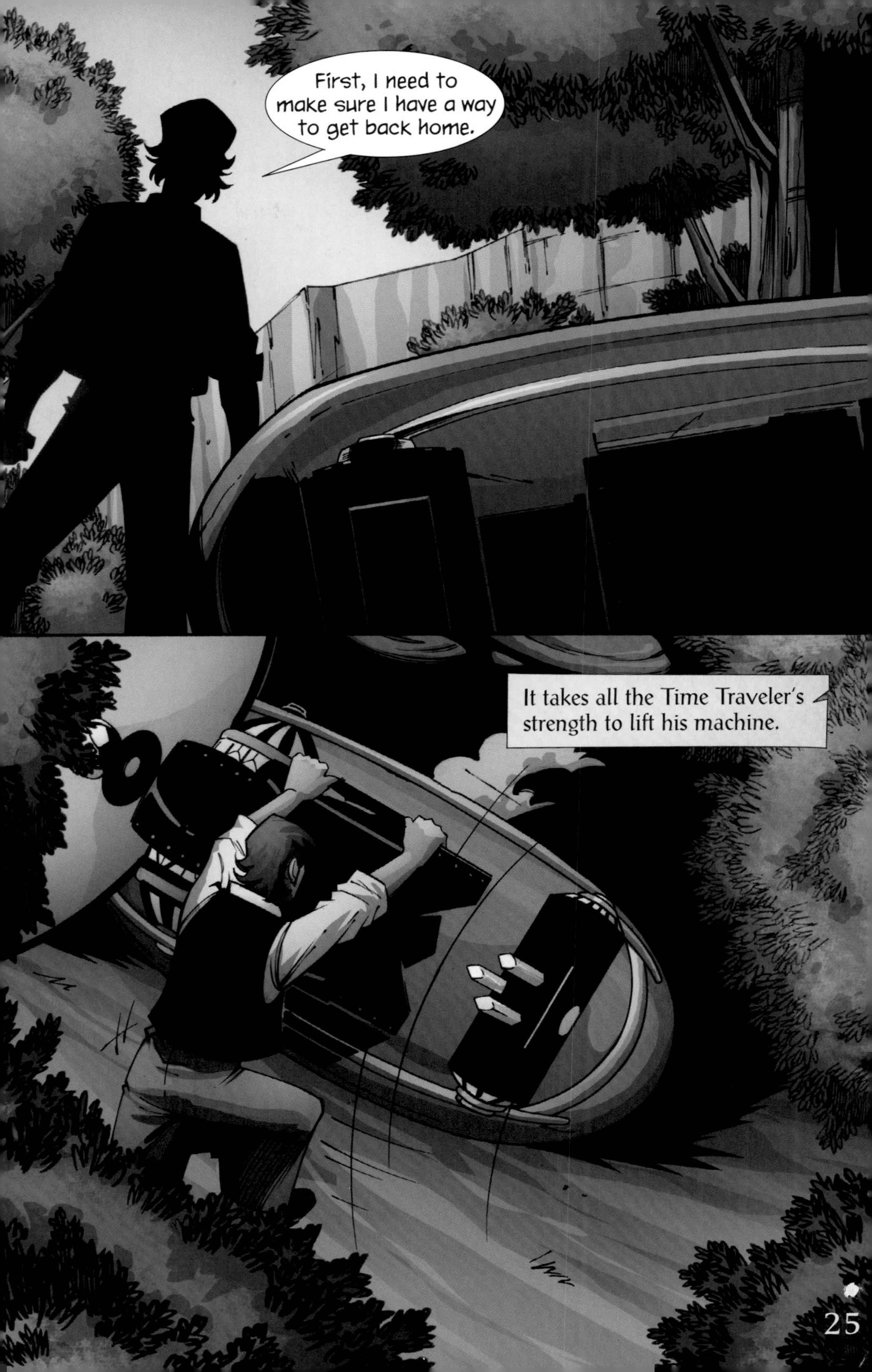
First, I need to make sure I have a way to get back home.
It takes all the Time Traveler's strength to lift his machine.

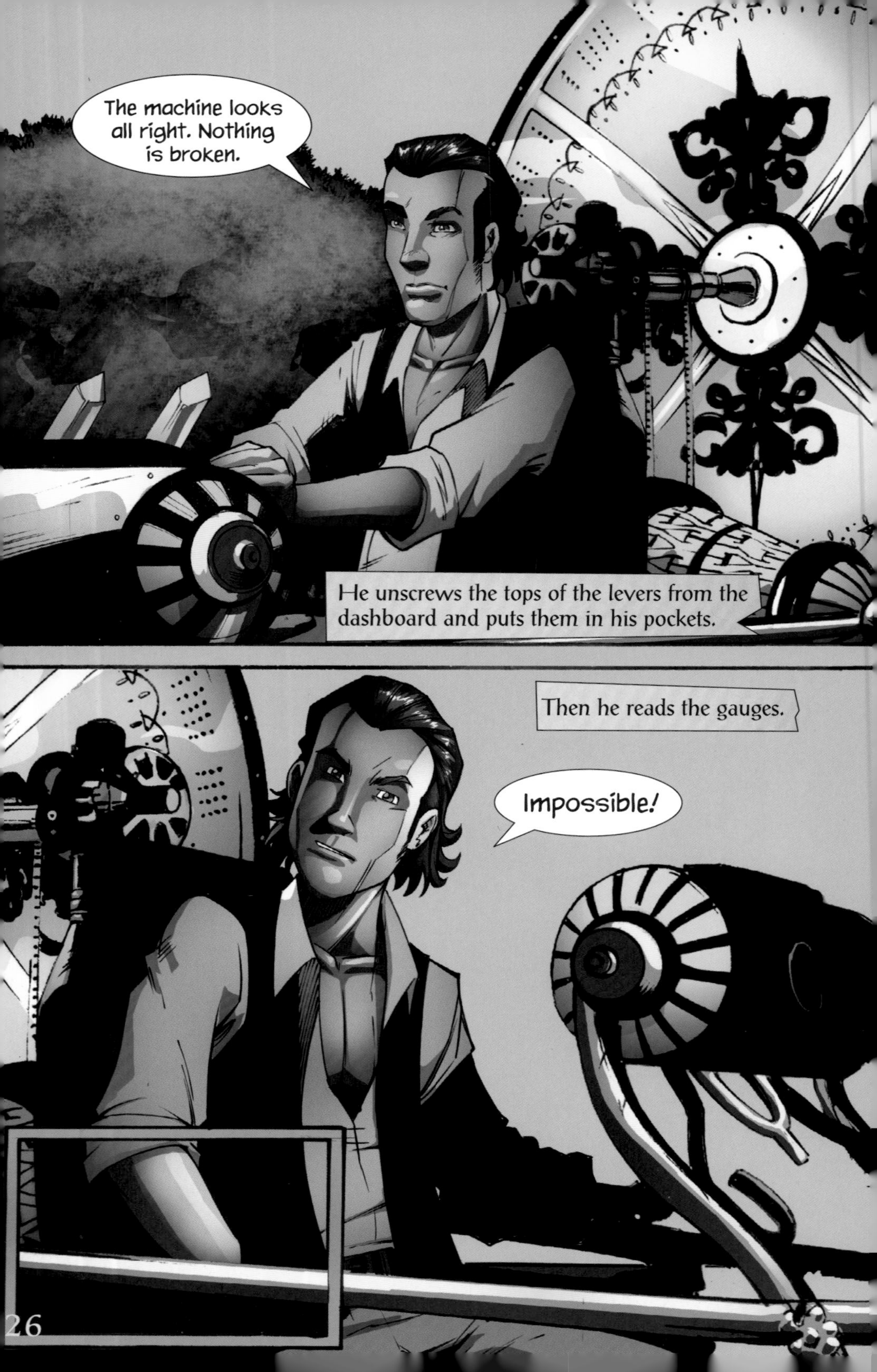
The machine looks all right. Nothing is broken.
He unscrews the tops of the levers from the dashboard and puts them in his pockets.
Then he reads the gauges.
Impossible!

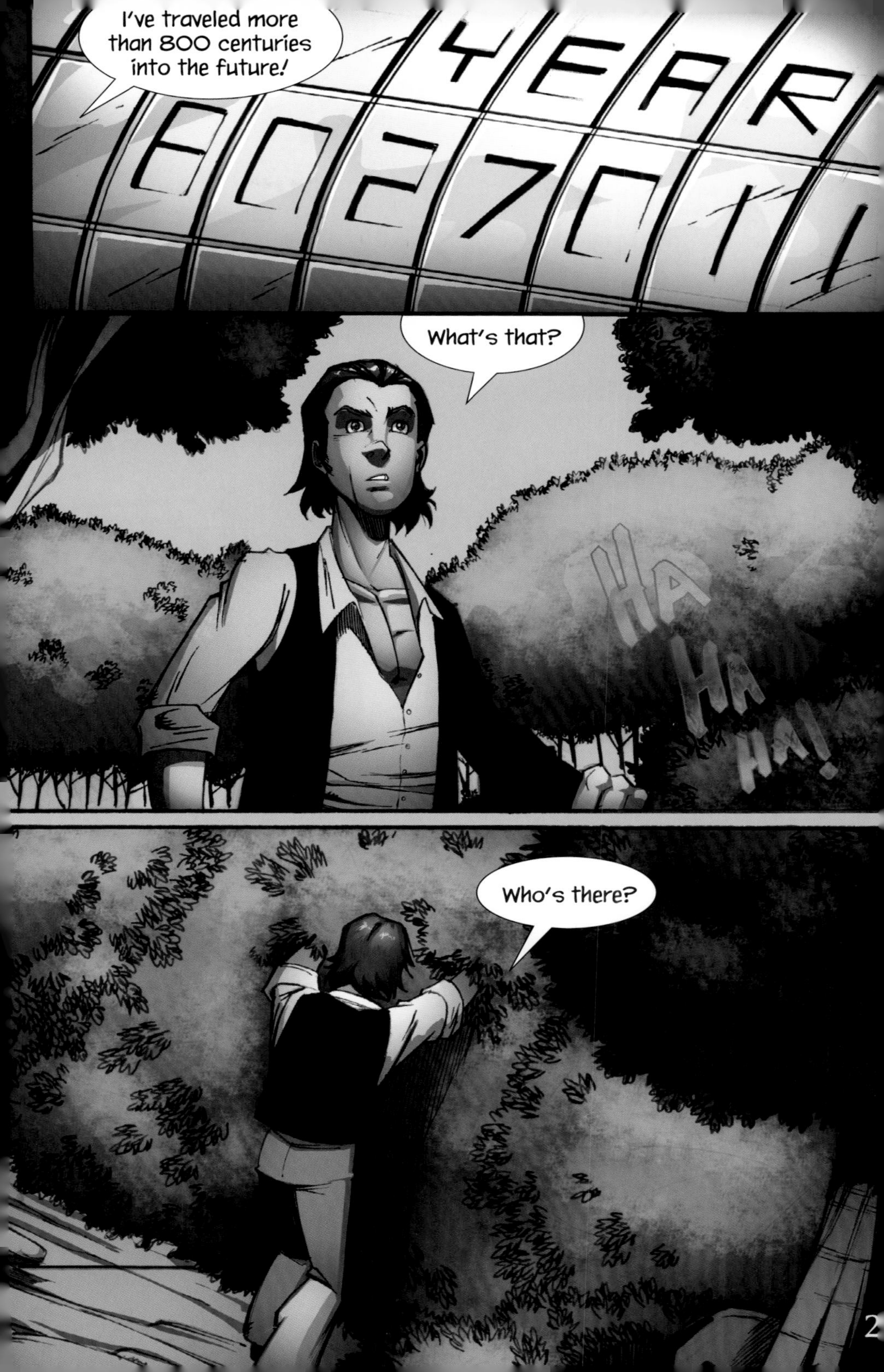
I've traveled more than 800 centuries into the future!
YEAR
802701
What's that?
HA HA HA!
Who's there?

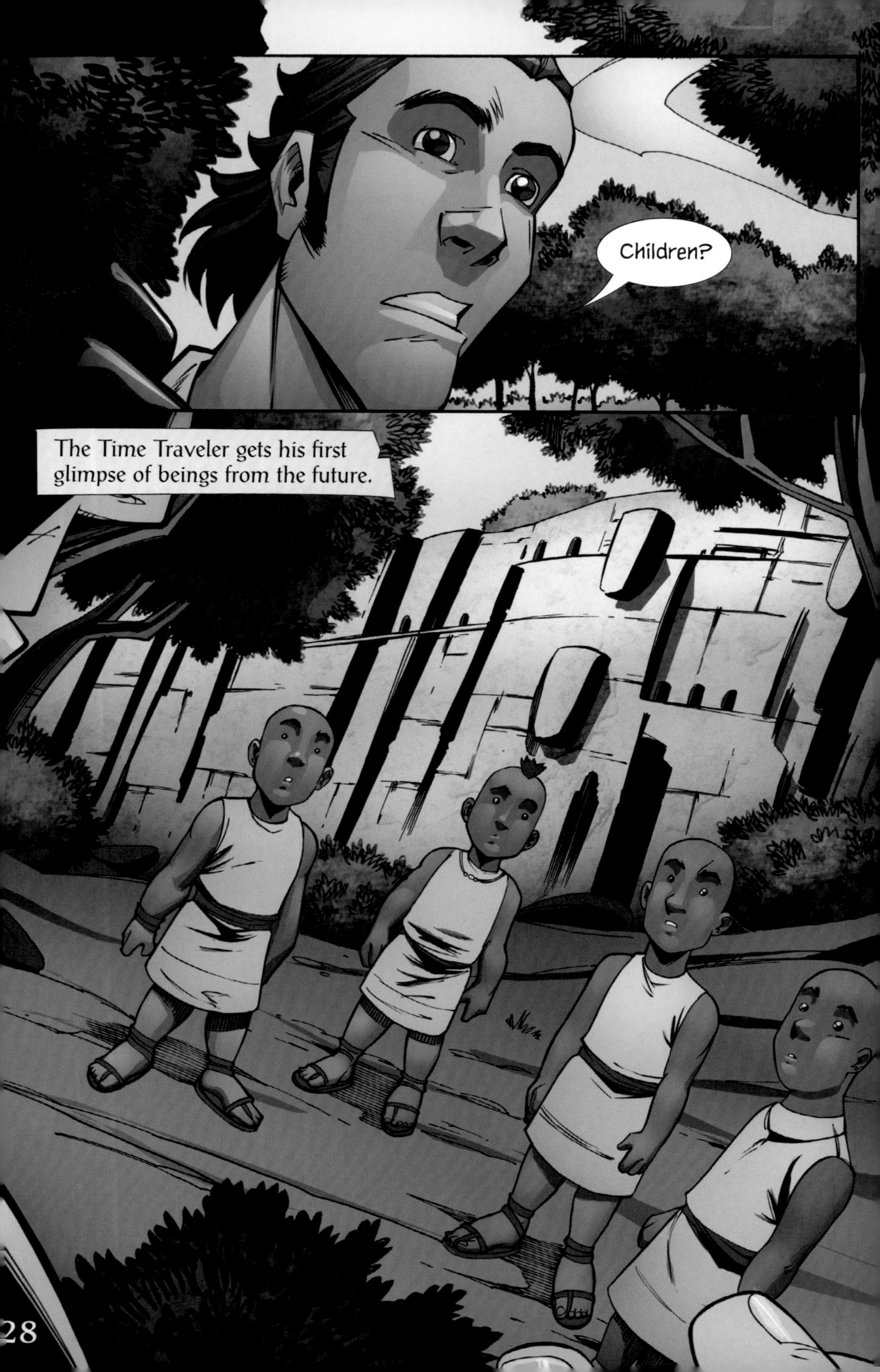
Children?
The Time Traveler gets his first glimpse of beings from the future.

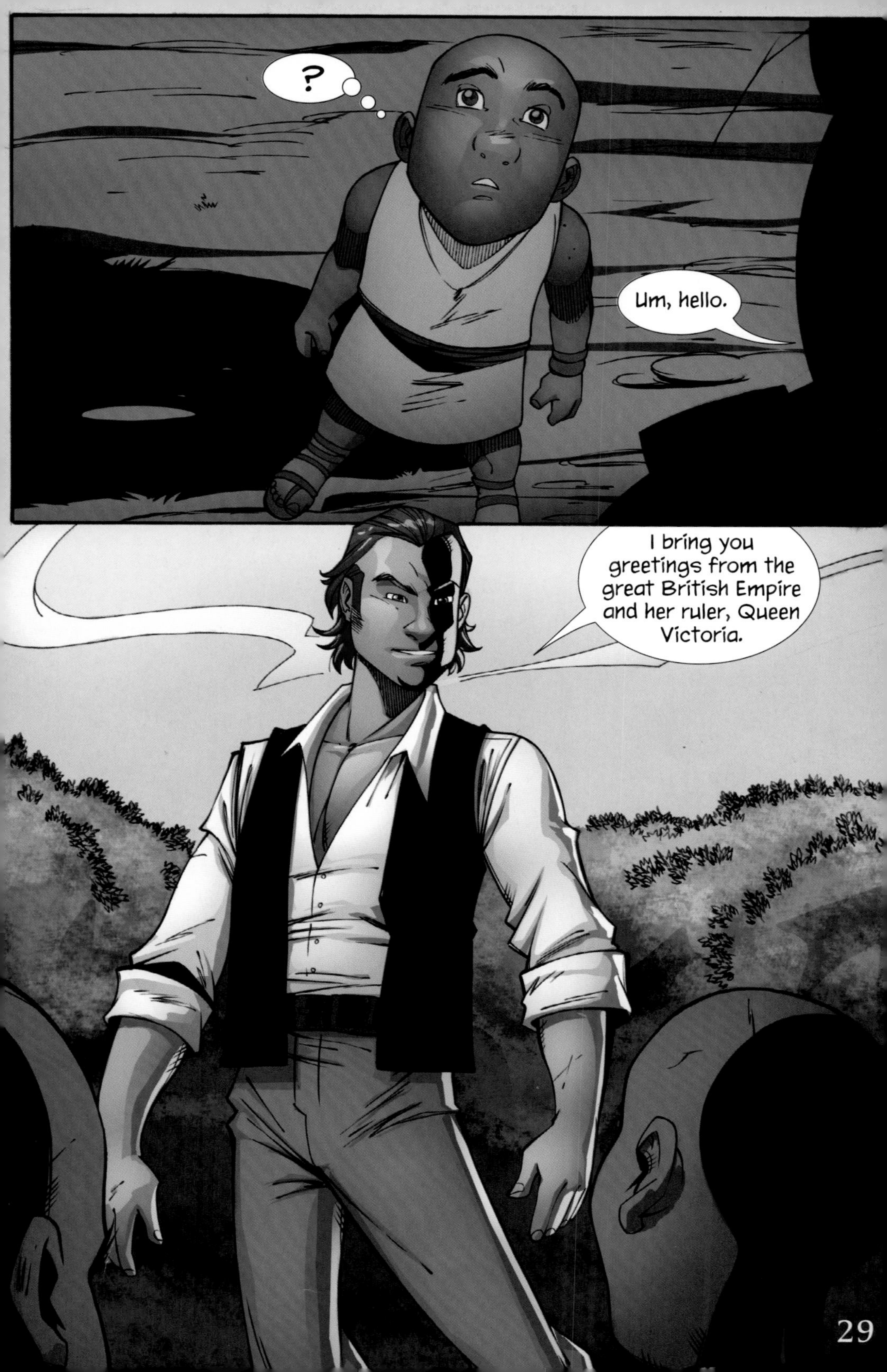
?
Um, hello.
I bring you greetings from the great British Empire and her ruler, Queen Victoria.

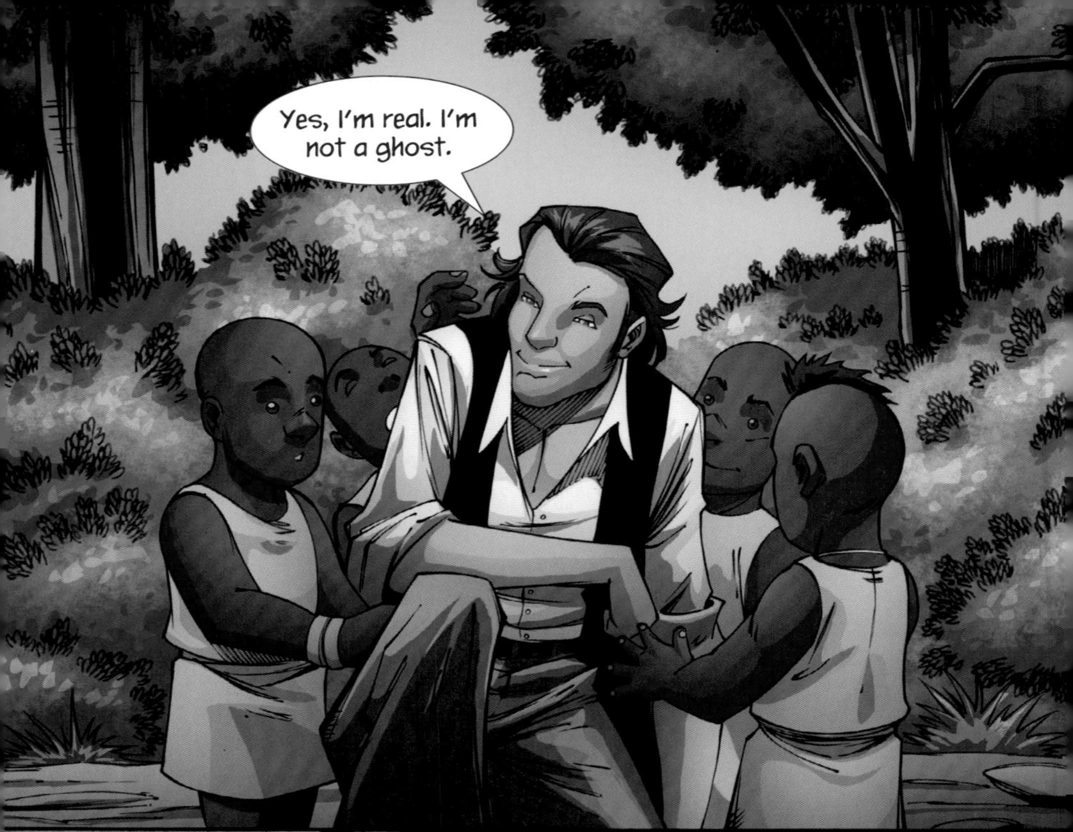
Yes, I'm real. I'm not a ghost.

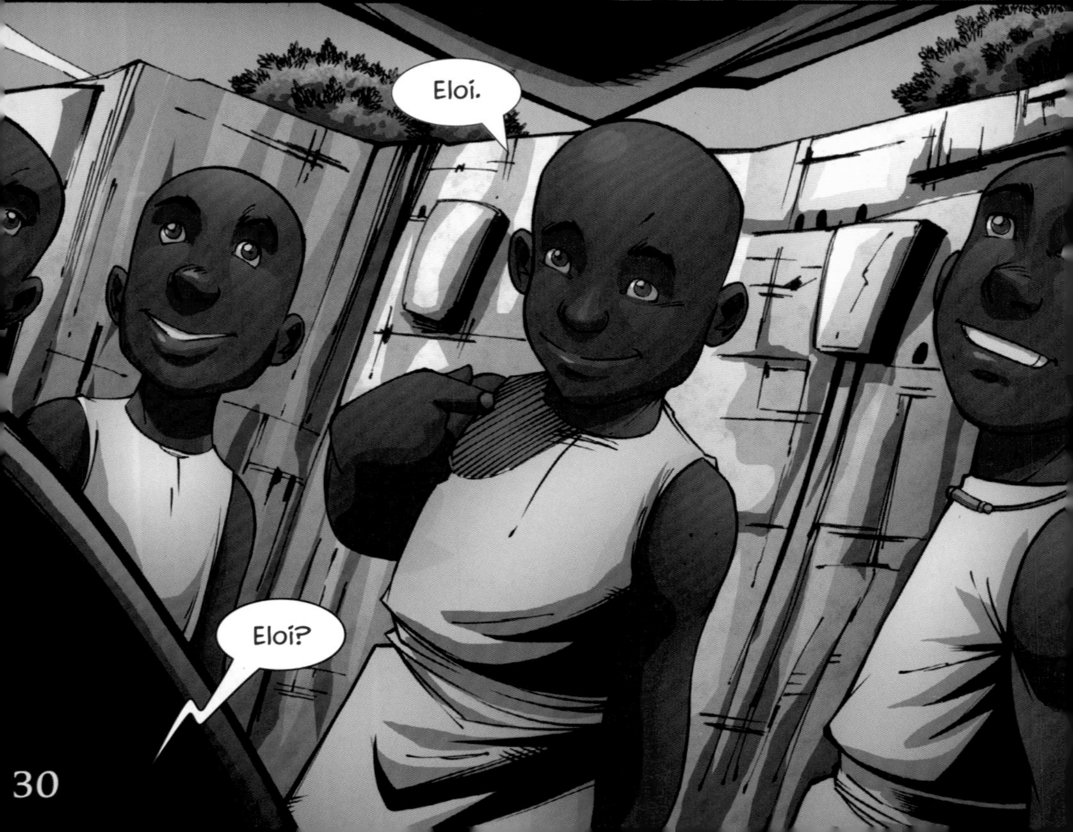
Eloi.
Eloi?

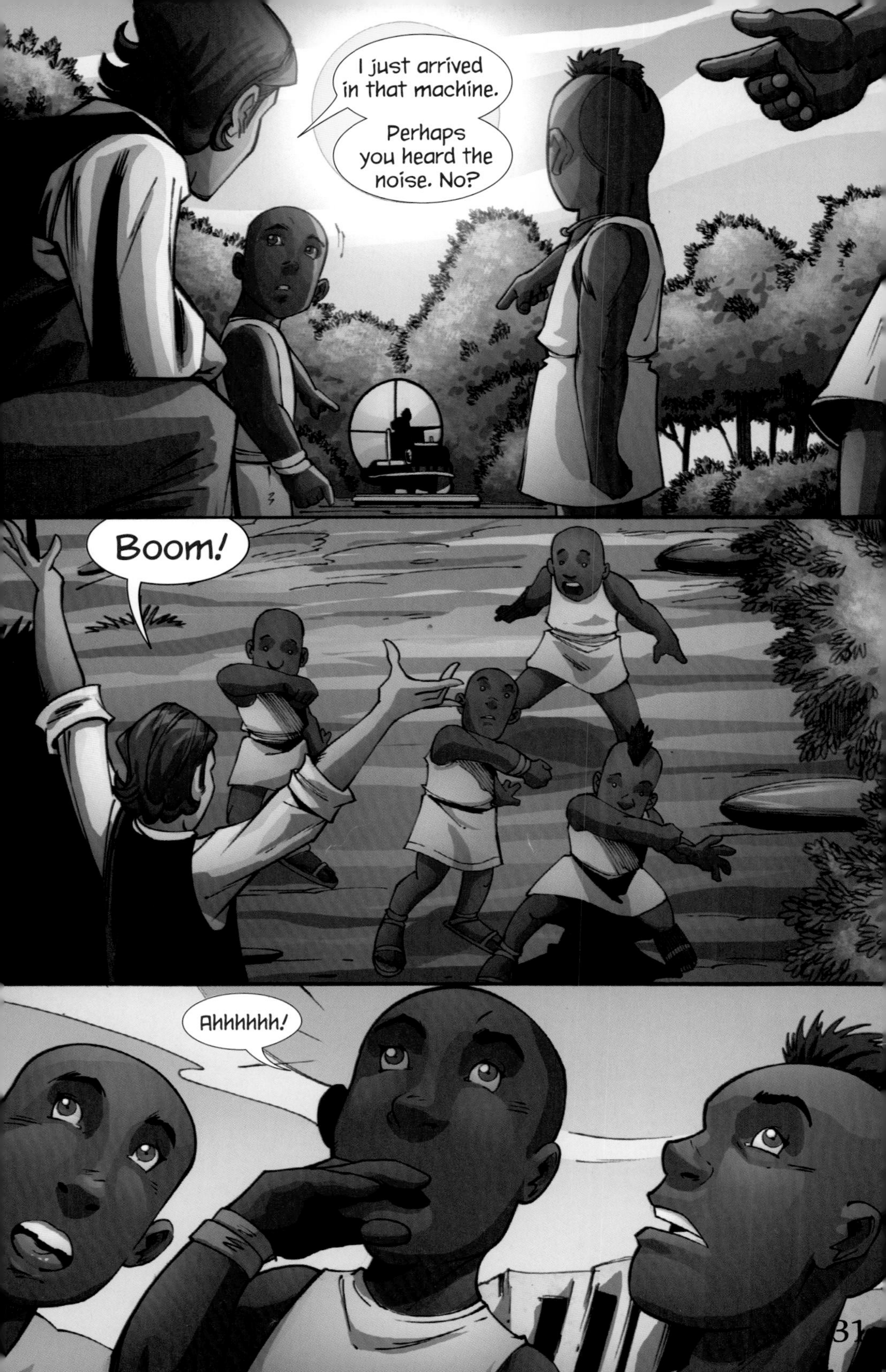
I just arrived in that machine.
Perhaps you heard the noise. No?
Boom!
Ahhhhhh!

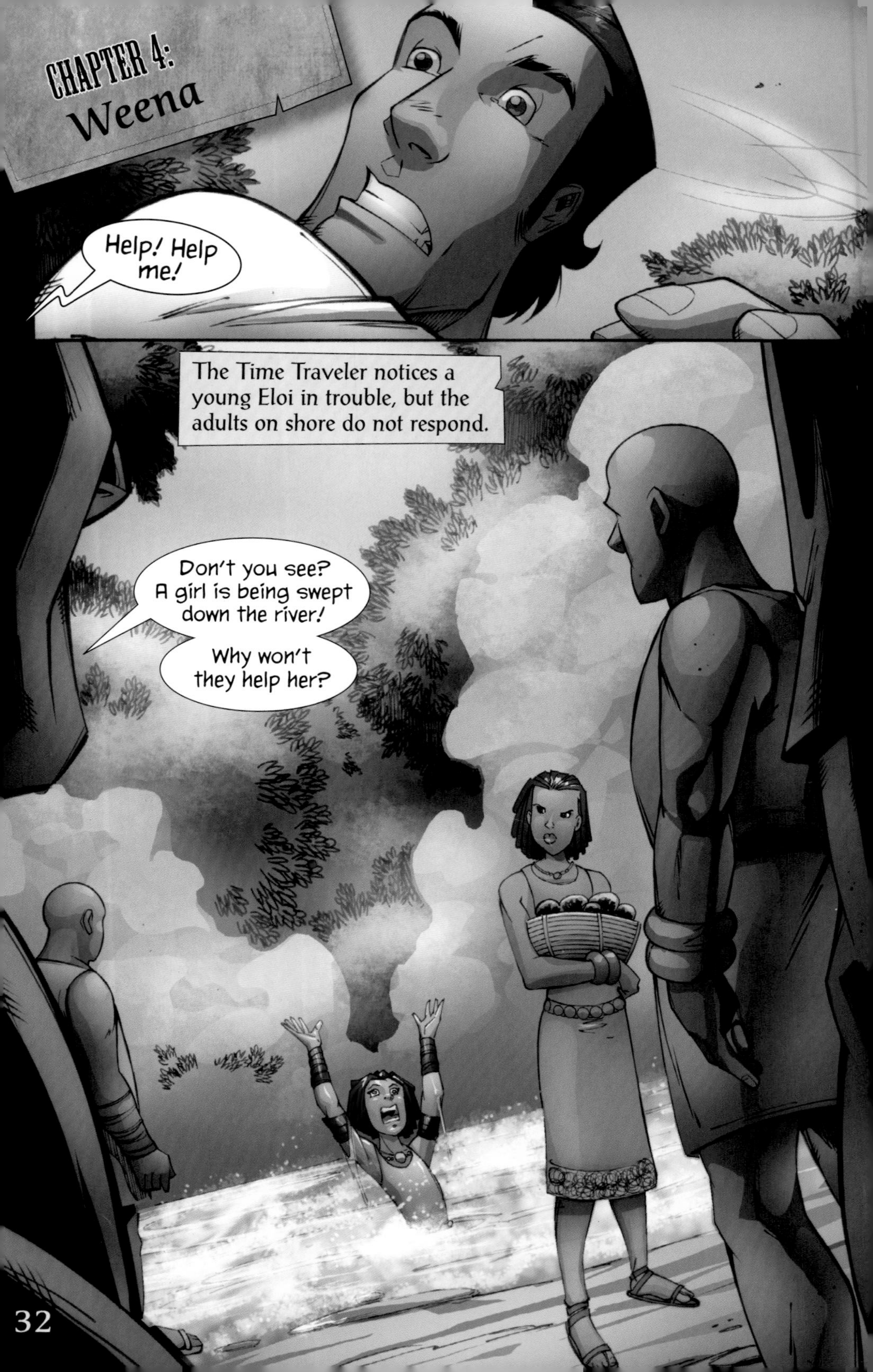
CHAPTER 4:
Weena
Help! Help me!
The Time Traveler notices a young Eloi in trouble, but the adults on shore do not respond.
Don't you see? A girl is being swept down the river!
Why won't they help her?

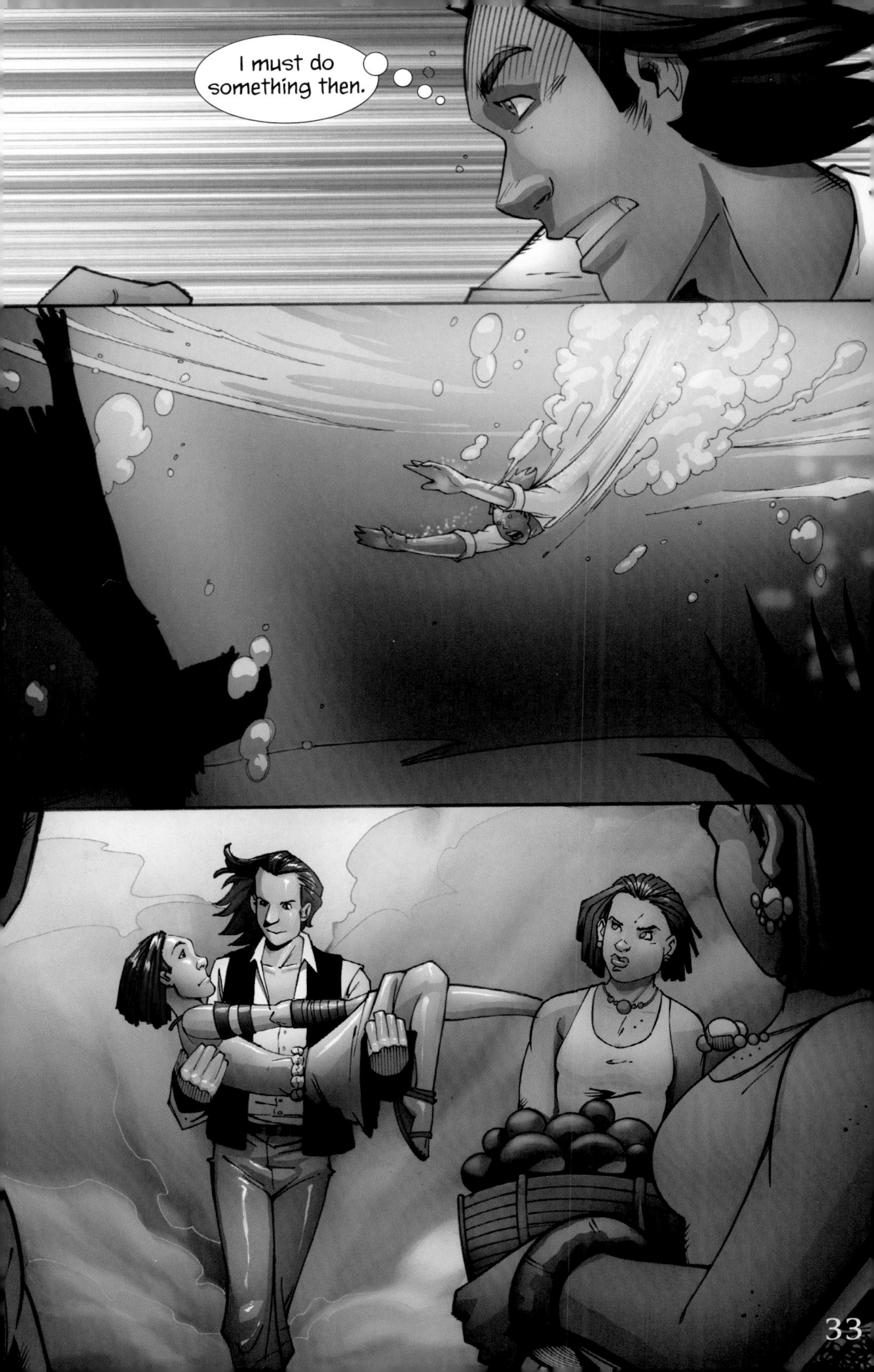
I must do something then.

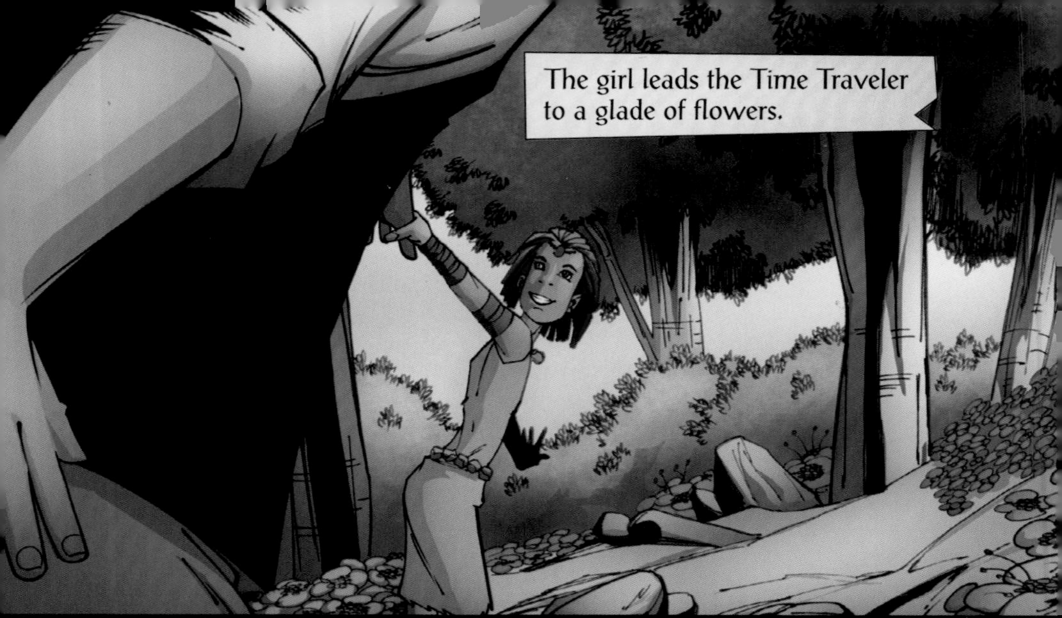
The girl leads the Time Traveler to a glade of flowers.

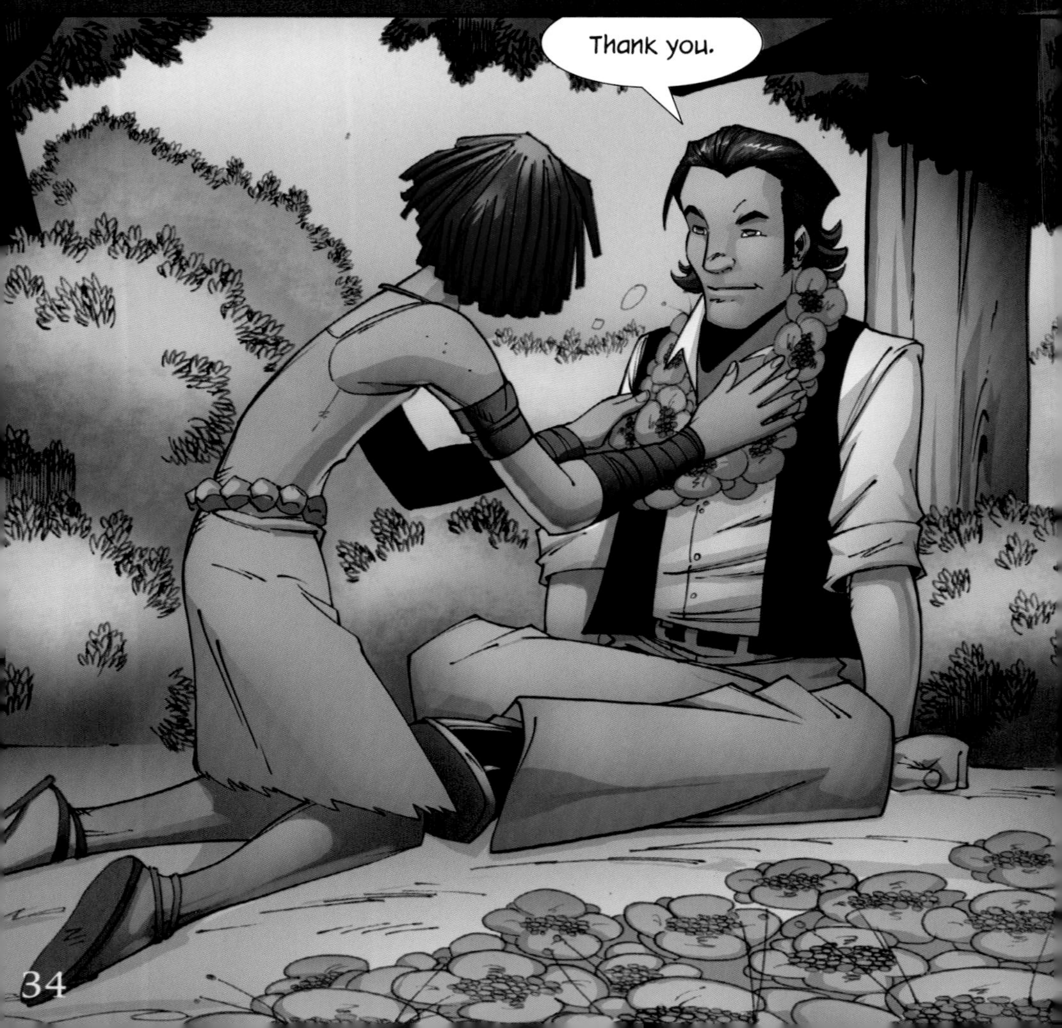
Thank you.

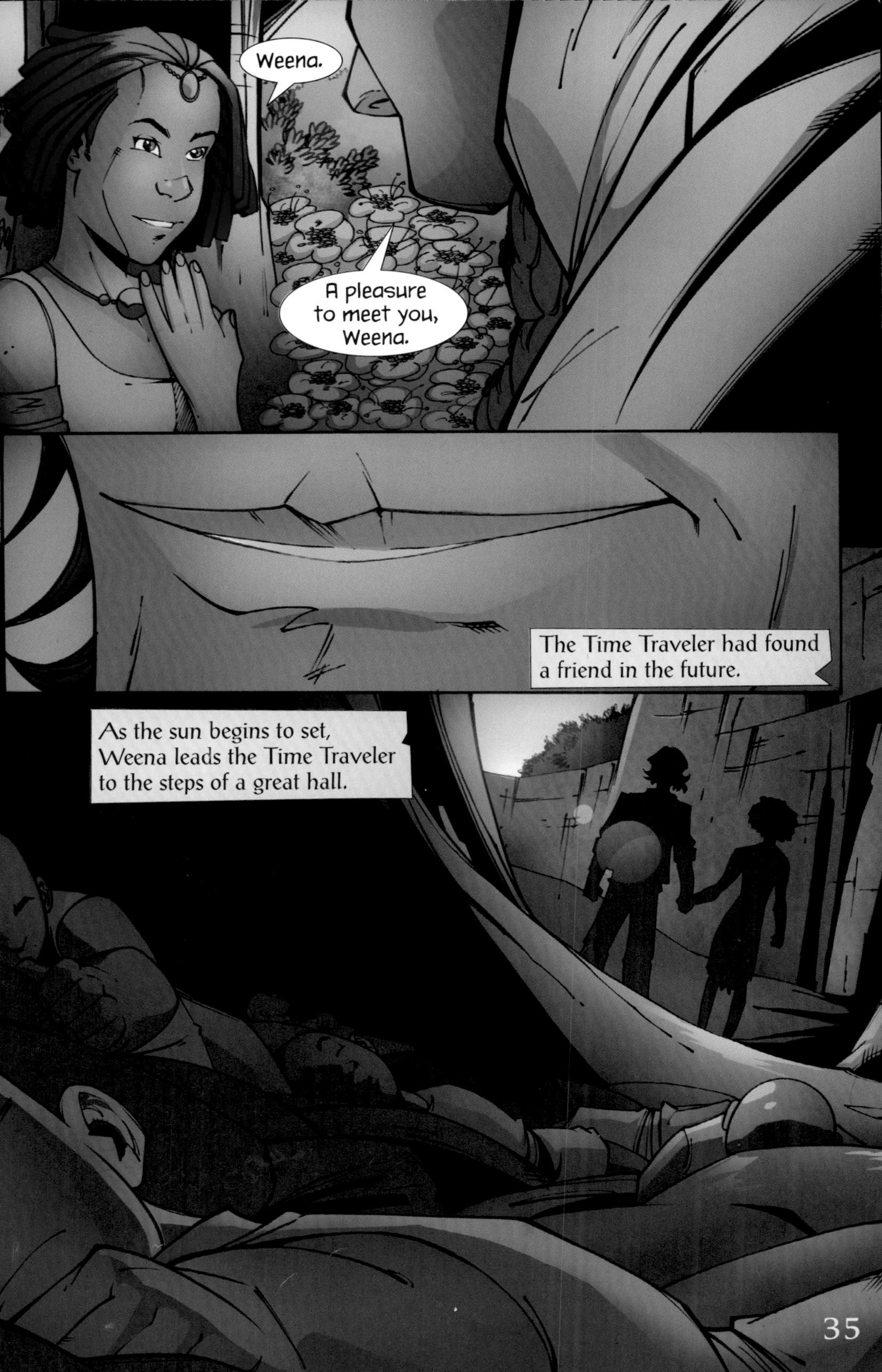

Weena.
A pleasure to meet you, Weena.
The Time Traveler had found a friend in the future.
As the sun begins to set, Weena leads the Time Traveler to the steps of a great hall.

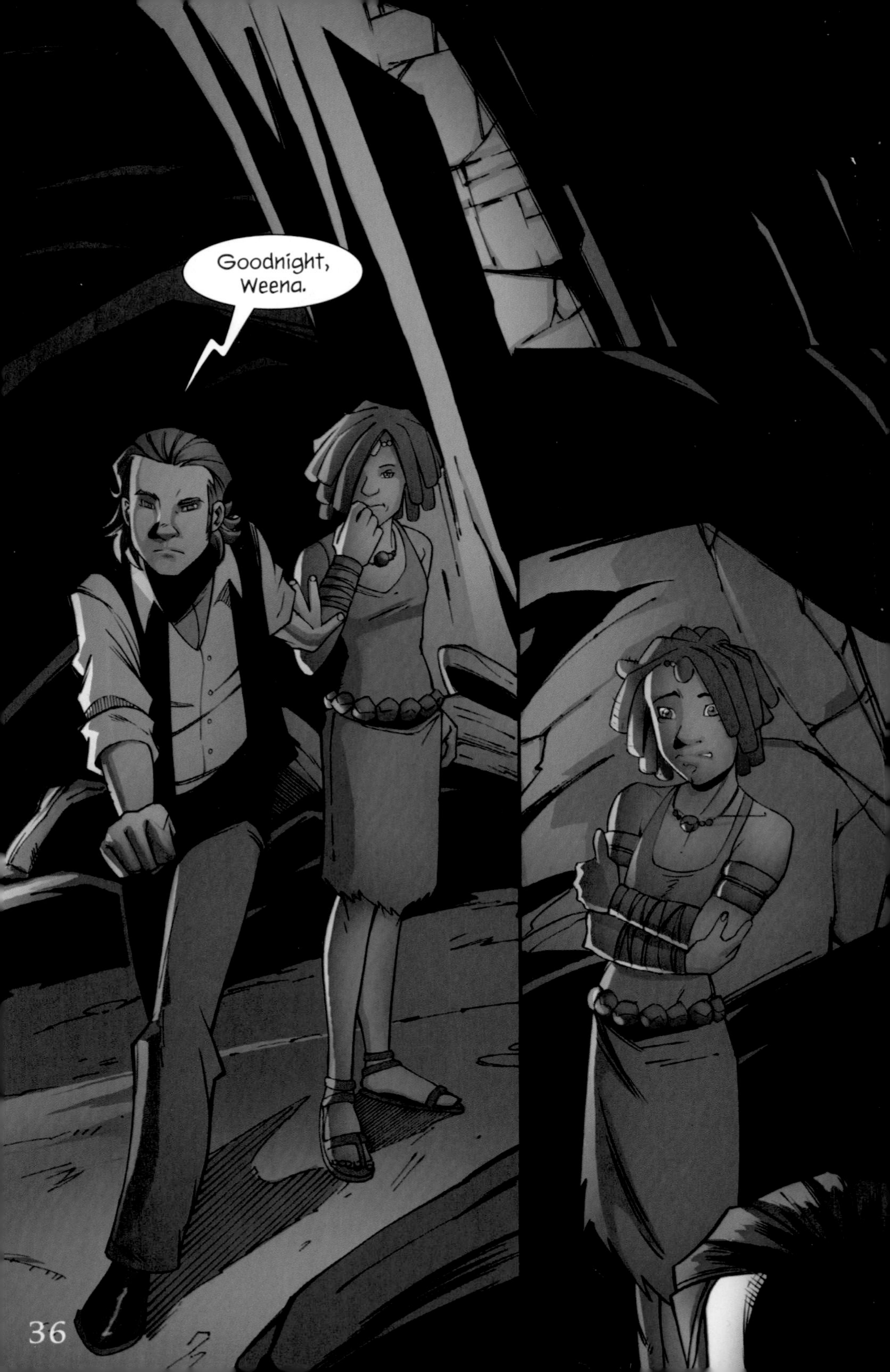
Goodnight, Weena.

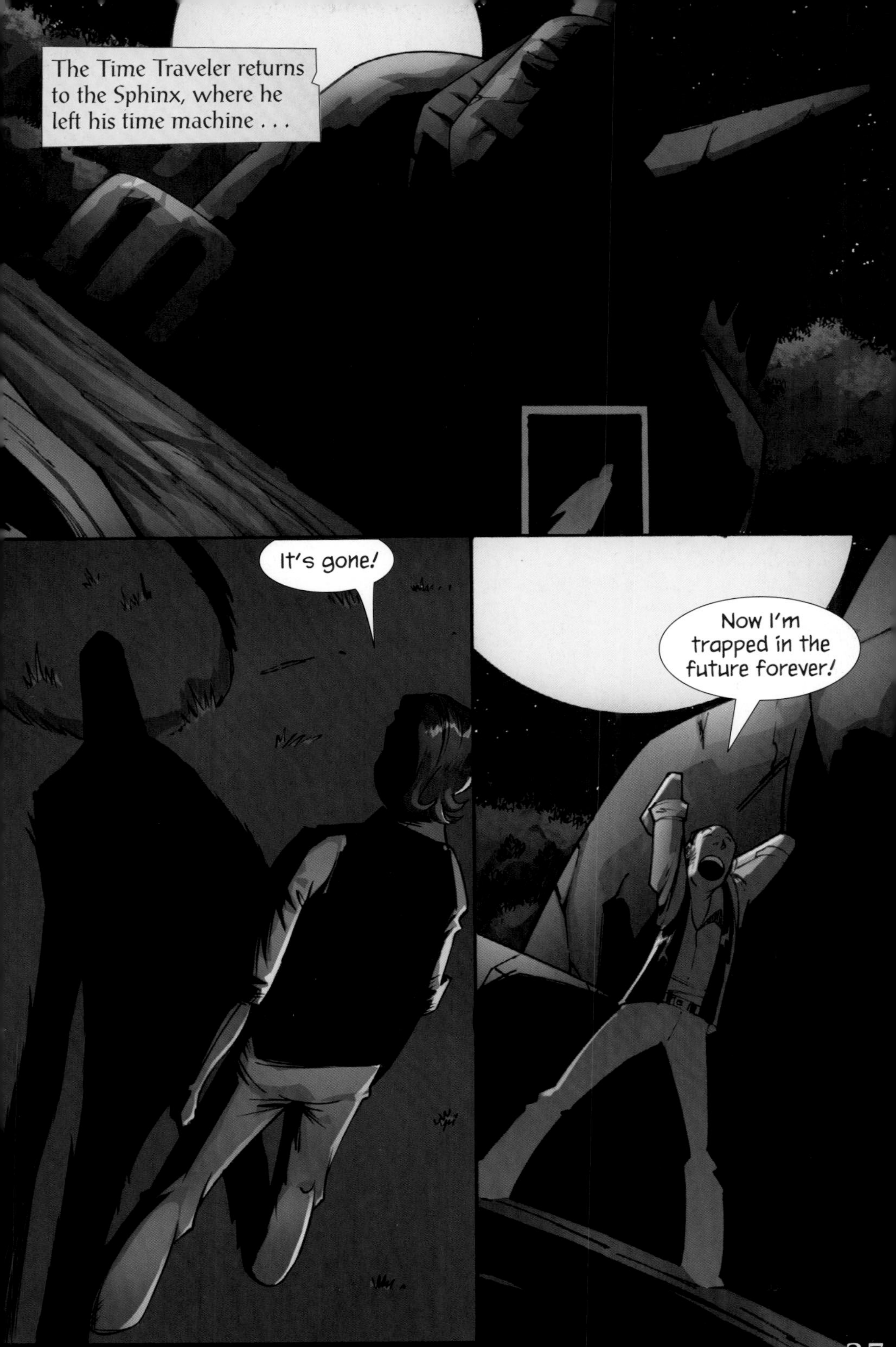
The Time Traveler returns to the Sphinx, where he left his time machine . . .
It's gone!
Now I'm trapped in the future forever!

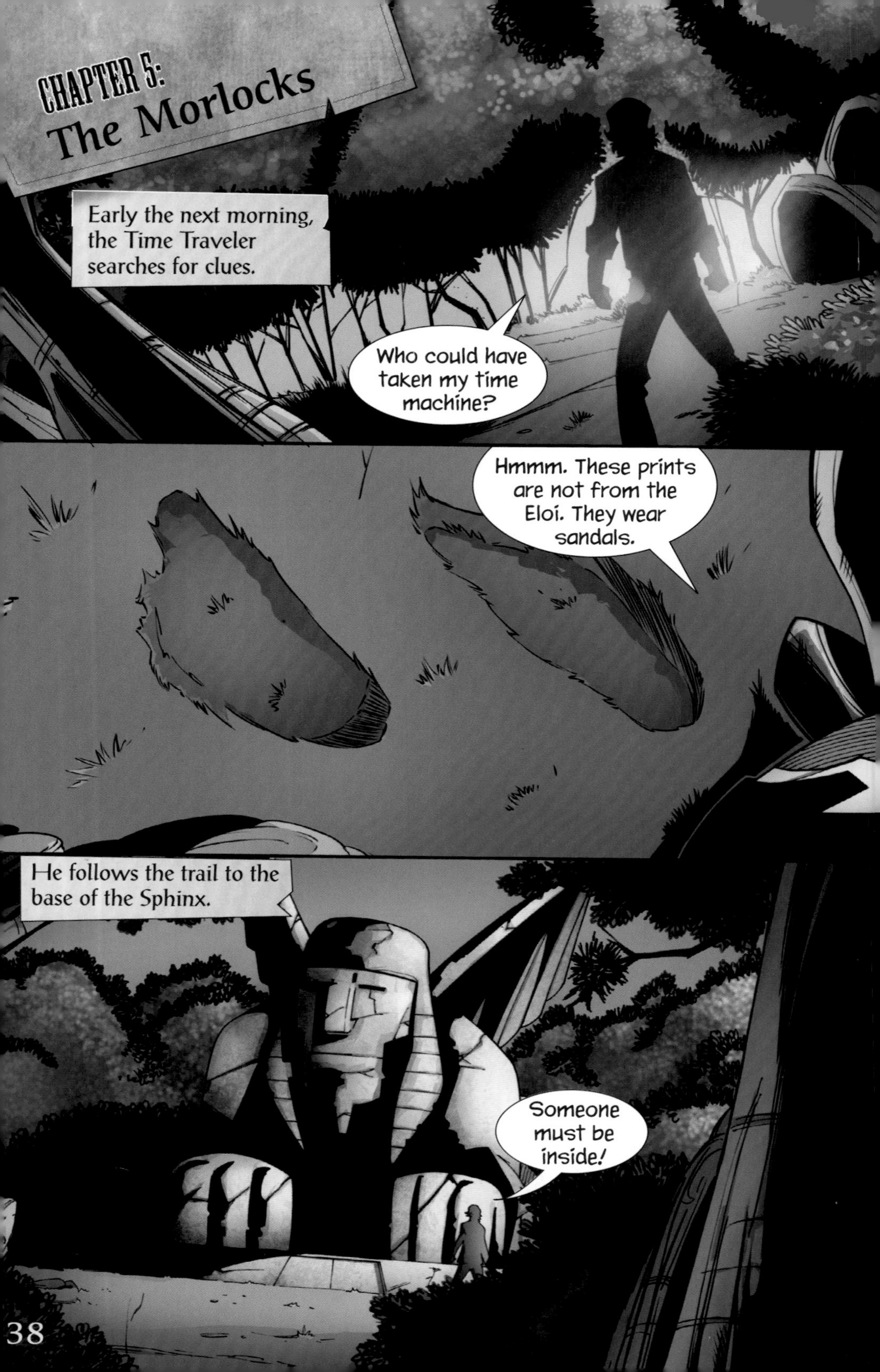
CHAPTER 5:
The Morlocks
Early the next morning, the Time Traveler searches for clues.
Who could have taken my time machine?
Hmmm. These prints are not from the Eloi. They wear sandals.
He follows the trail to the base of the Sphinx.
Someone must be inside!

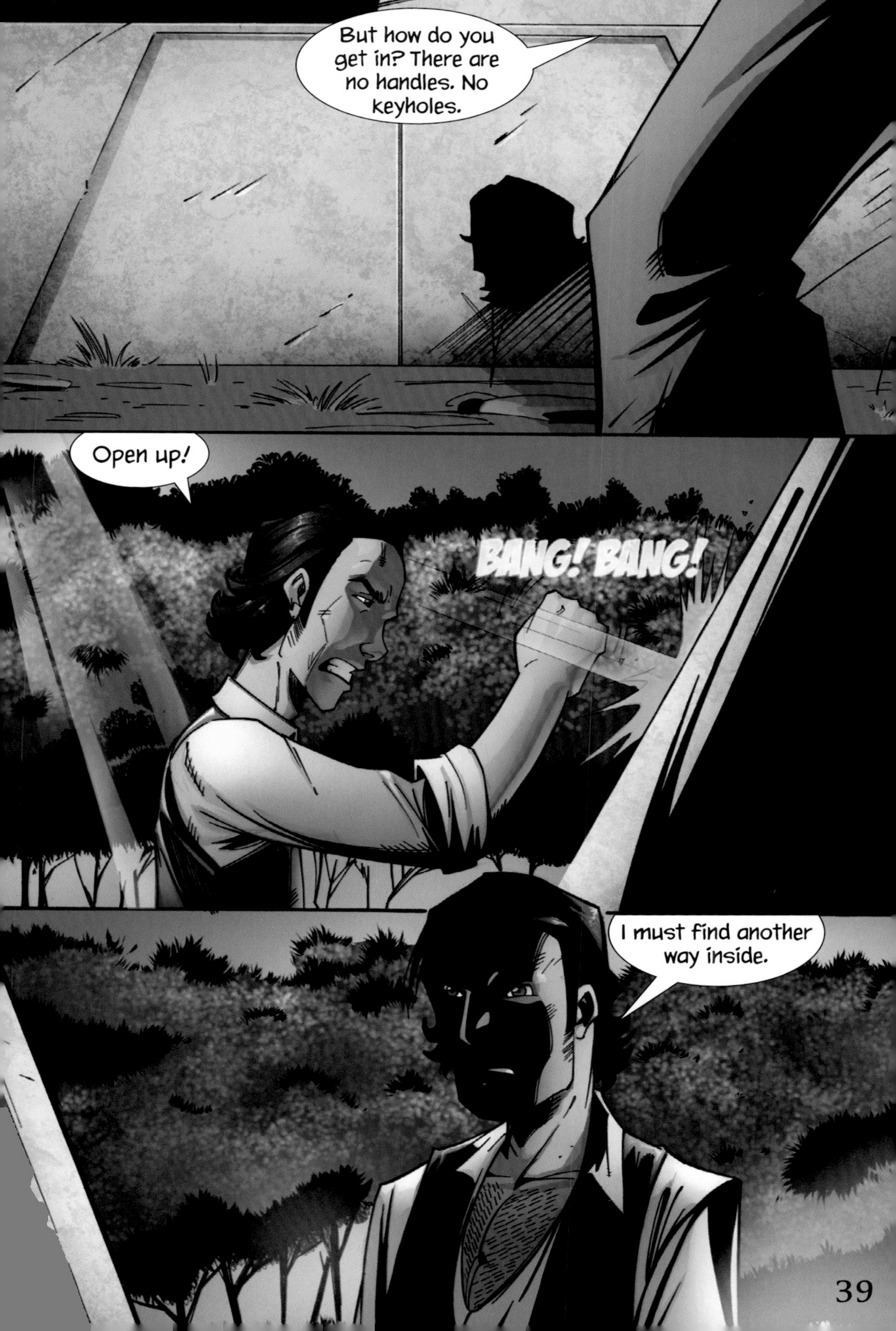
But how do you get in? There are no handles. No keyholes.
Open up!
BANG! BANG!
I must find another way inside.

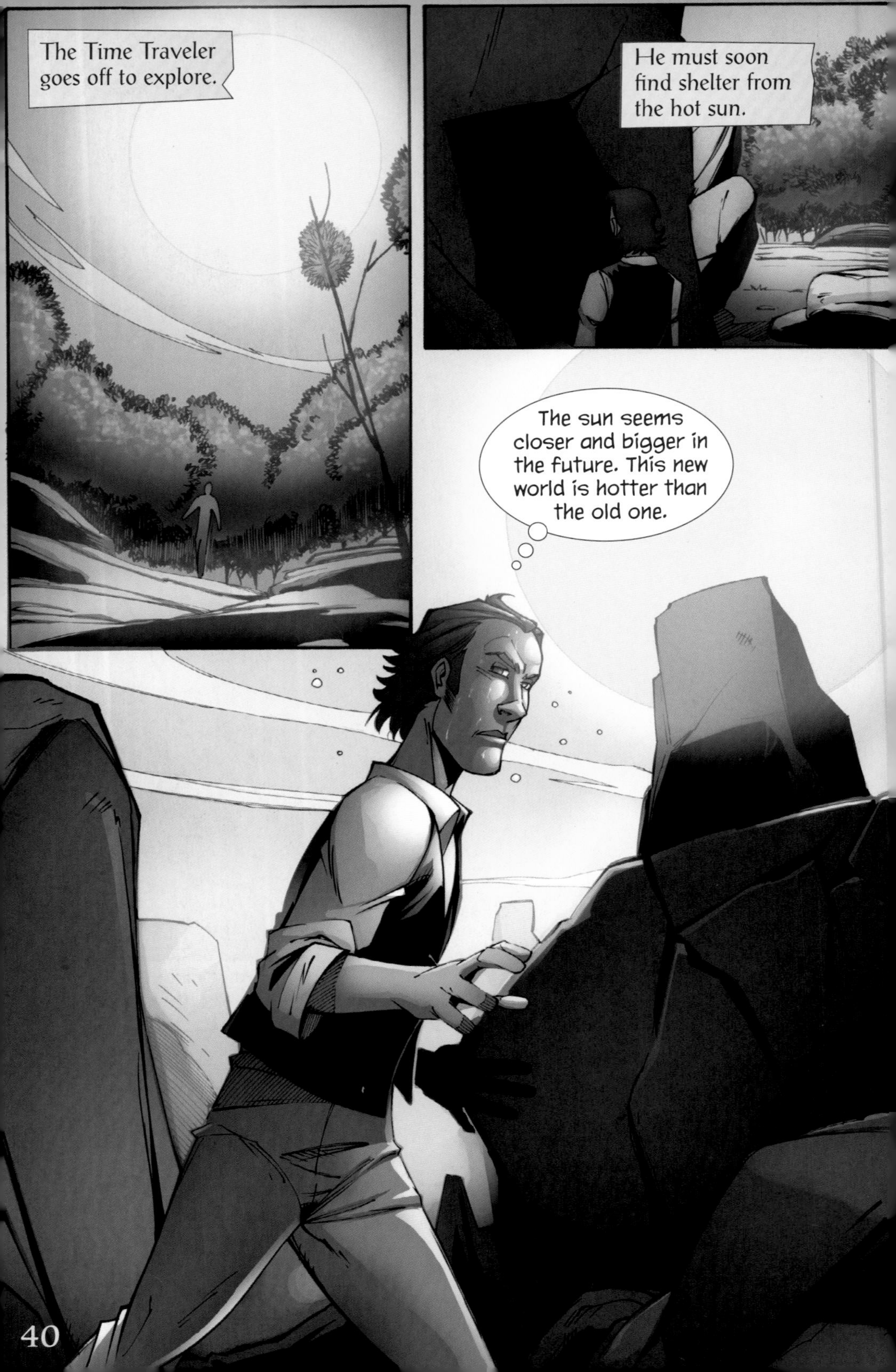

The Time Traveler goes off to explore.
He must soon find shelter from the hot sun.
The sun seems closer and bigger in the future. This new world is hotter than the old one.

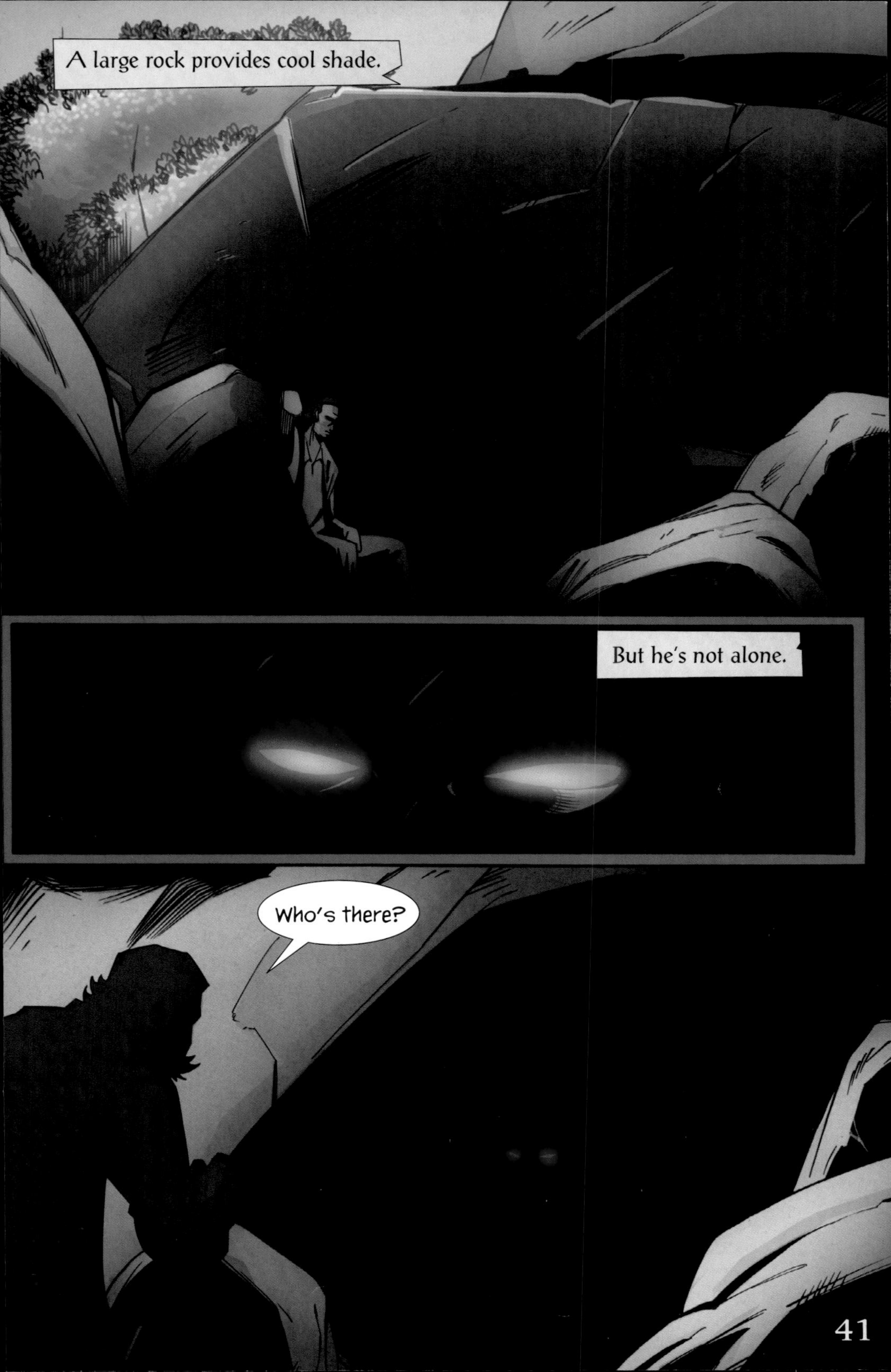
A large rock provides cool shade.
But he's not alone.
Who's there?

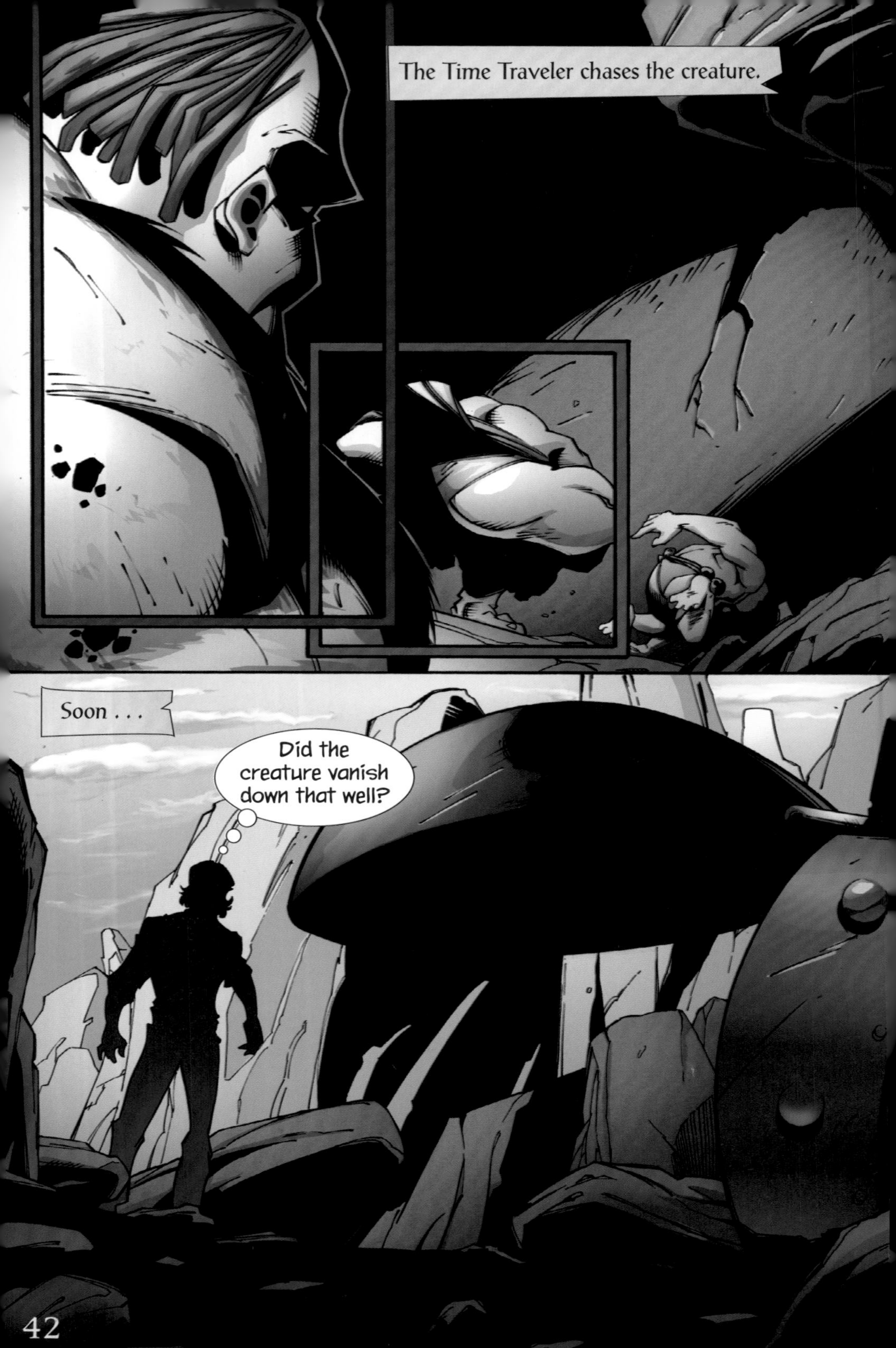
The Time Traveler chases the creature.
Soon . . .
Did the creature vanish down that well?

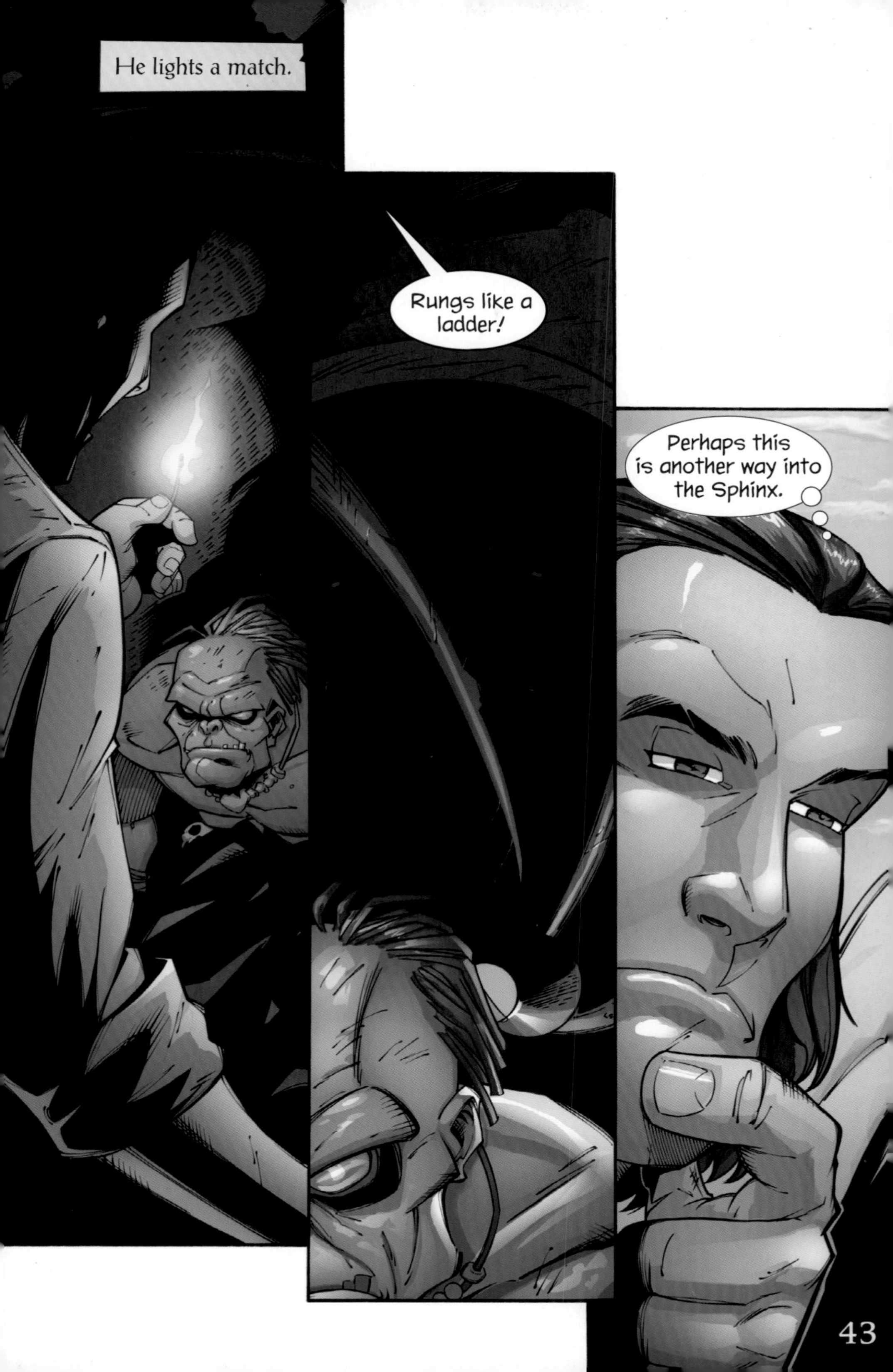
He lights a match.
Rungs like a ladder!
Perhaps this is another way into the Sphinx.

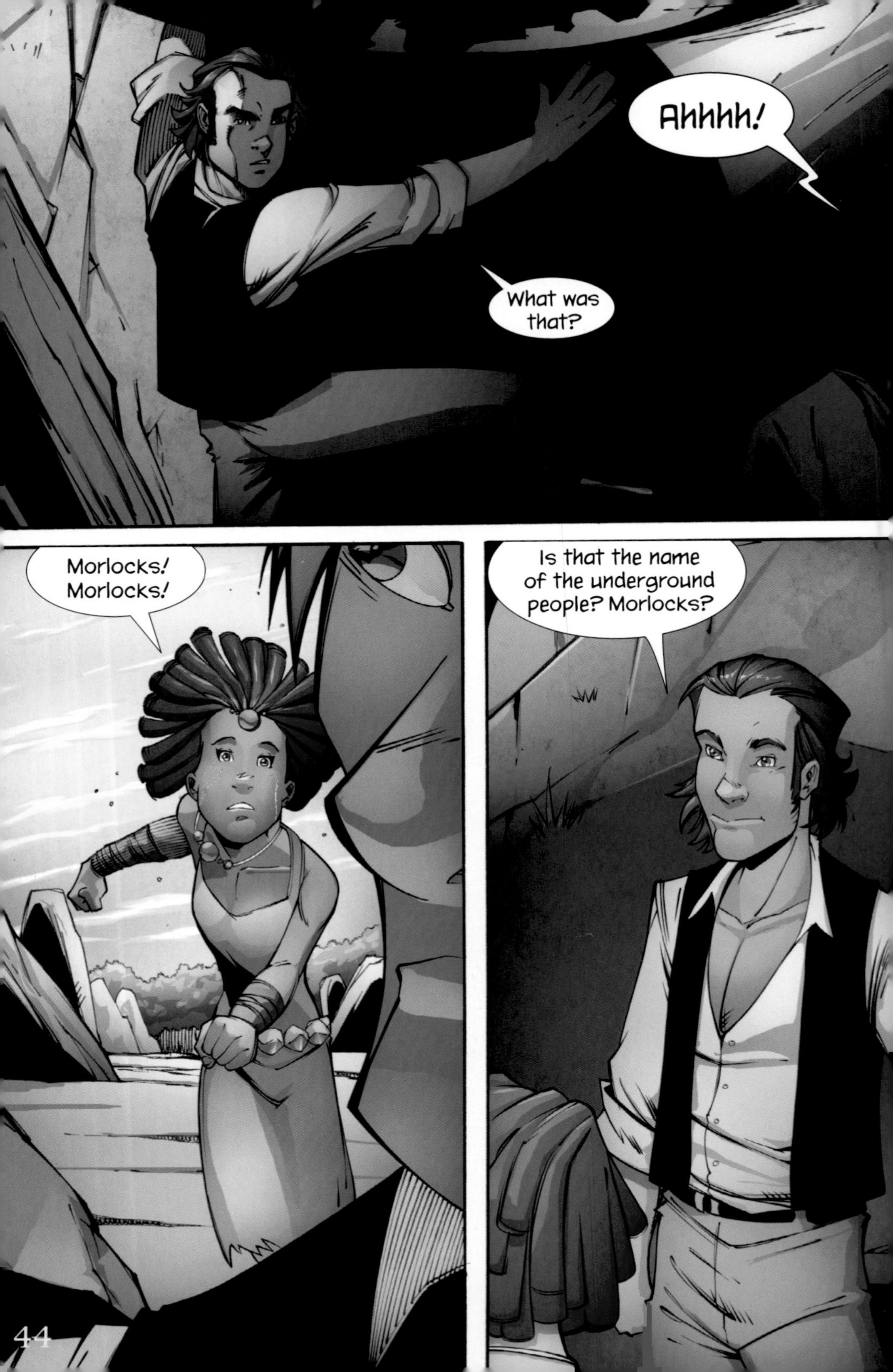
Ahhhh!
What was that?
Morlocks! Morlocks!
Is that the name of the underground people? Morlocks?

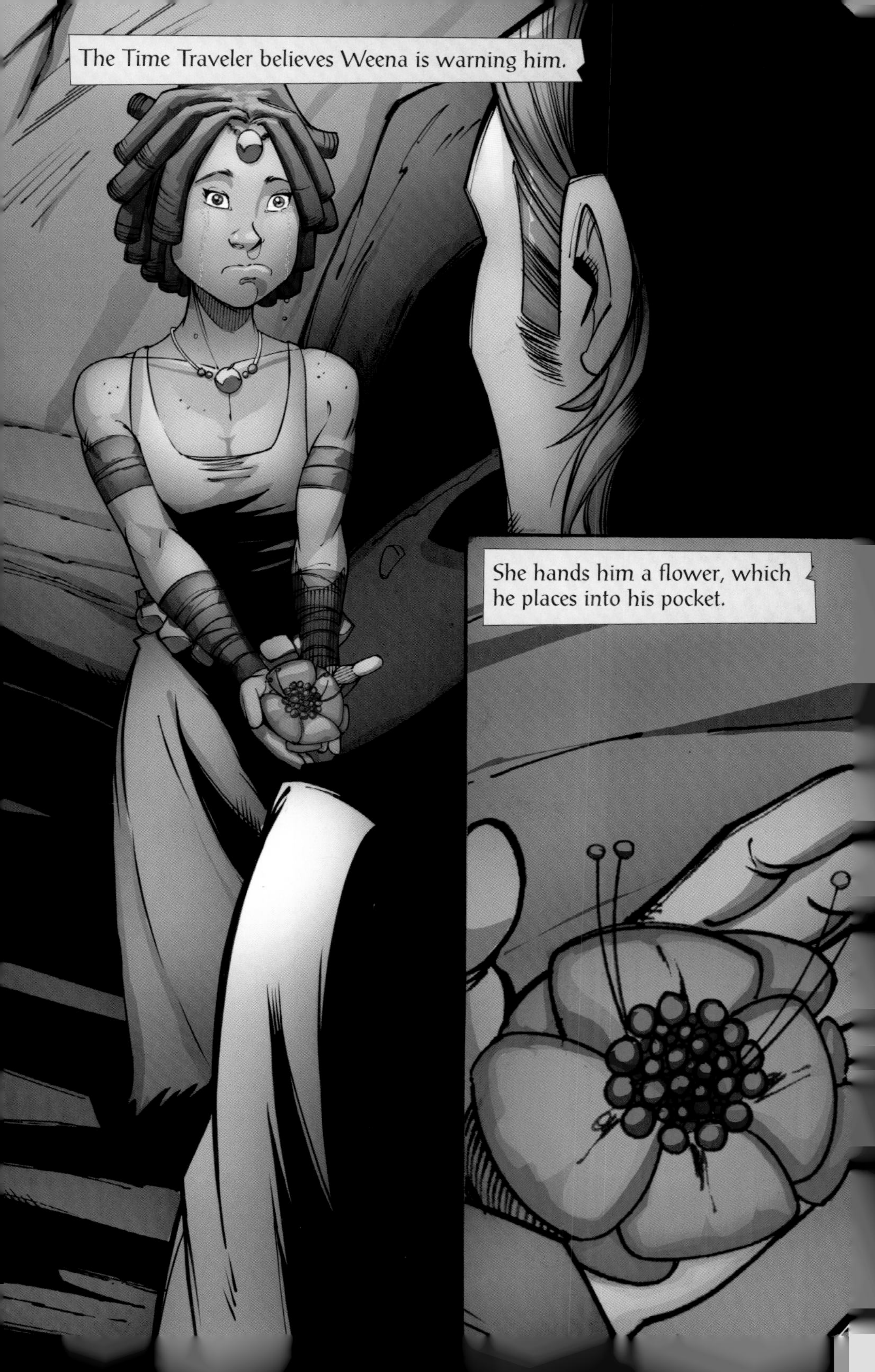
The Time Traveler believes Weena is warning him.
She hands him a flower, which he places into his pocket.

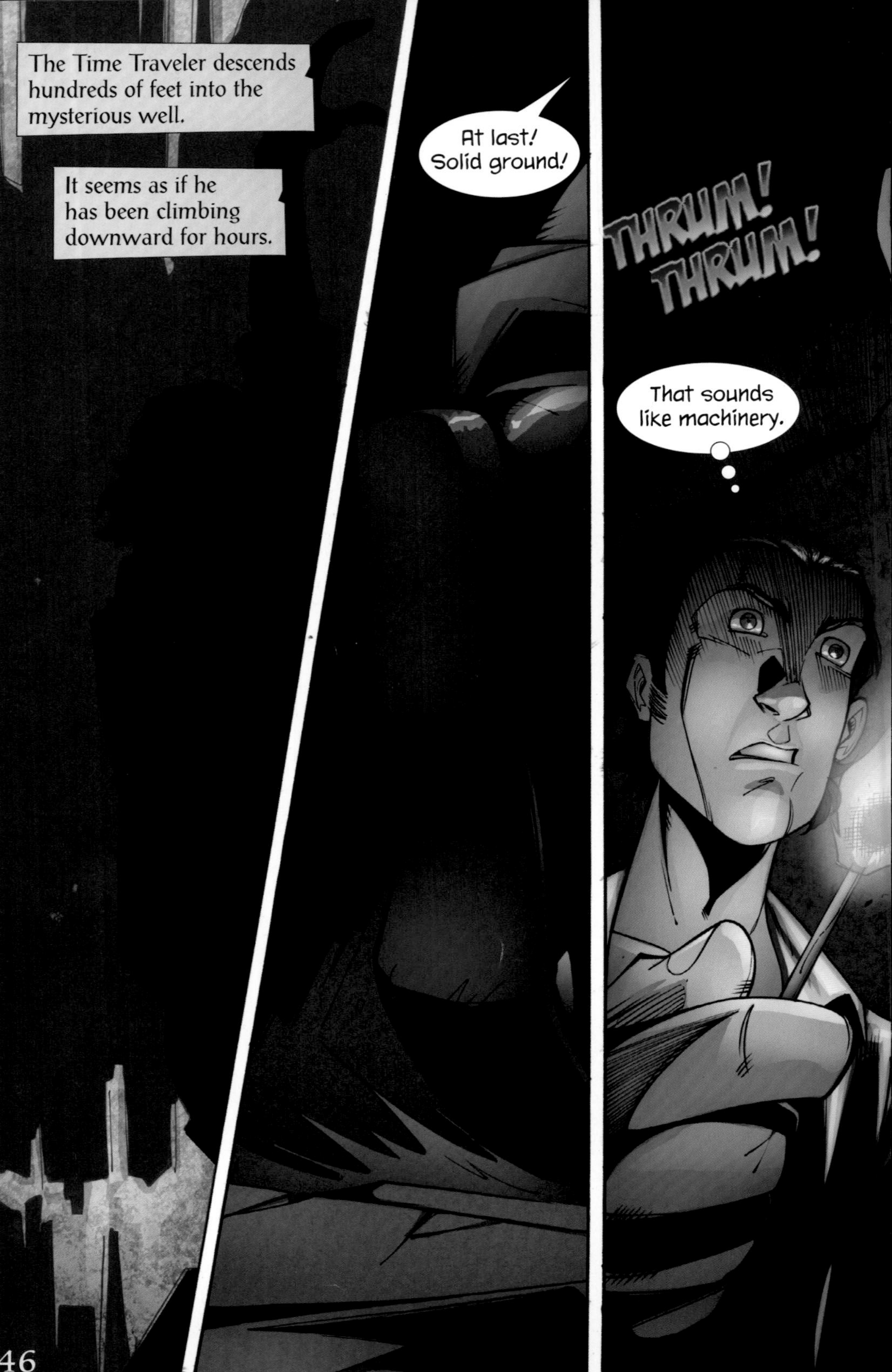

The Time Traveler descends hundreds of feet into the mysterious well.
It seems as if he has been climbing downward for hours.
At last! Solid ground!
THRUM! THRUM!
That sounds like machinery.

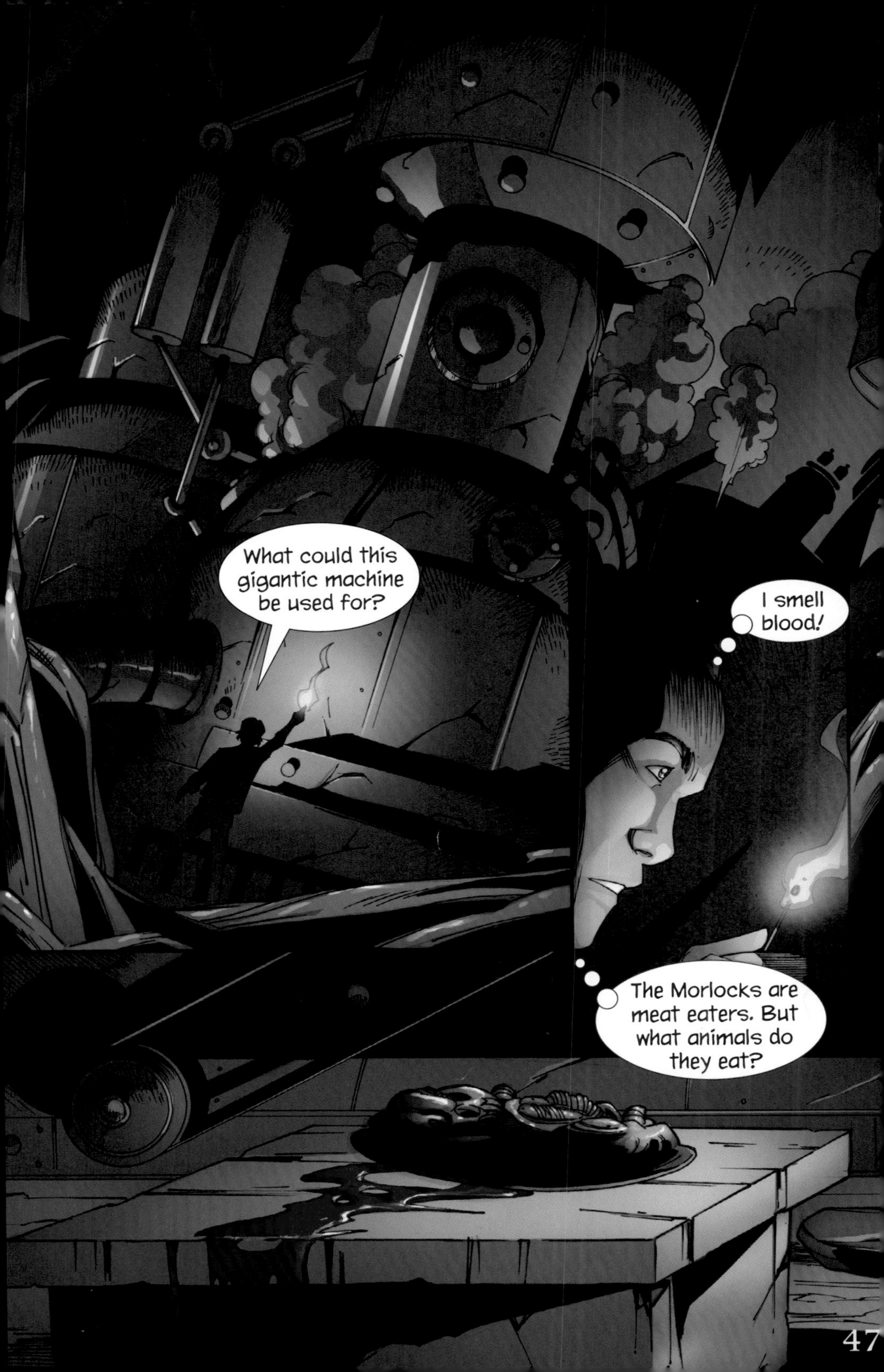
What could this gigantic machine be used for?
I smell blood!
The Morlocks are meat eaters. But what animals do they eat?

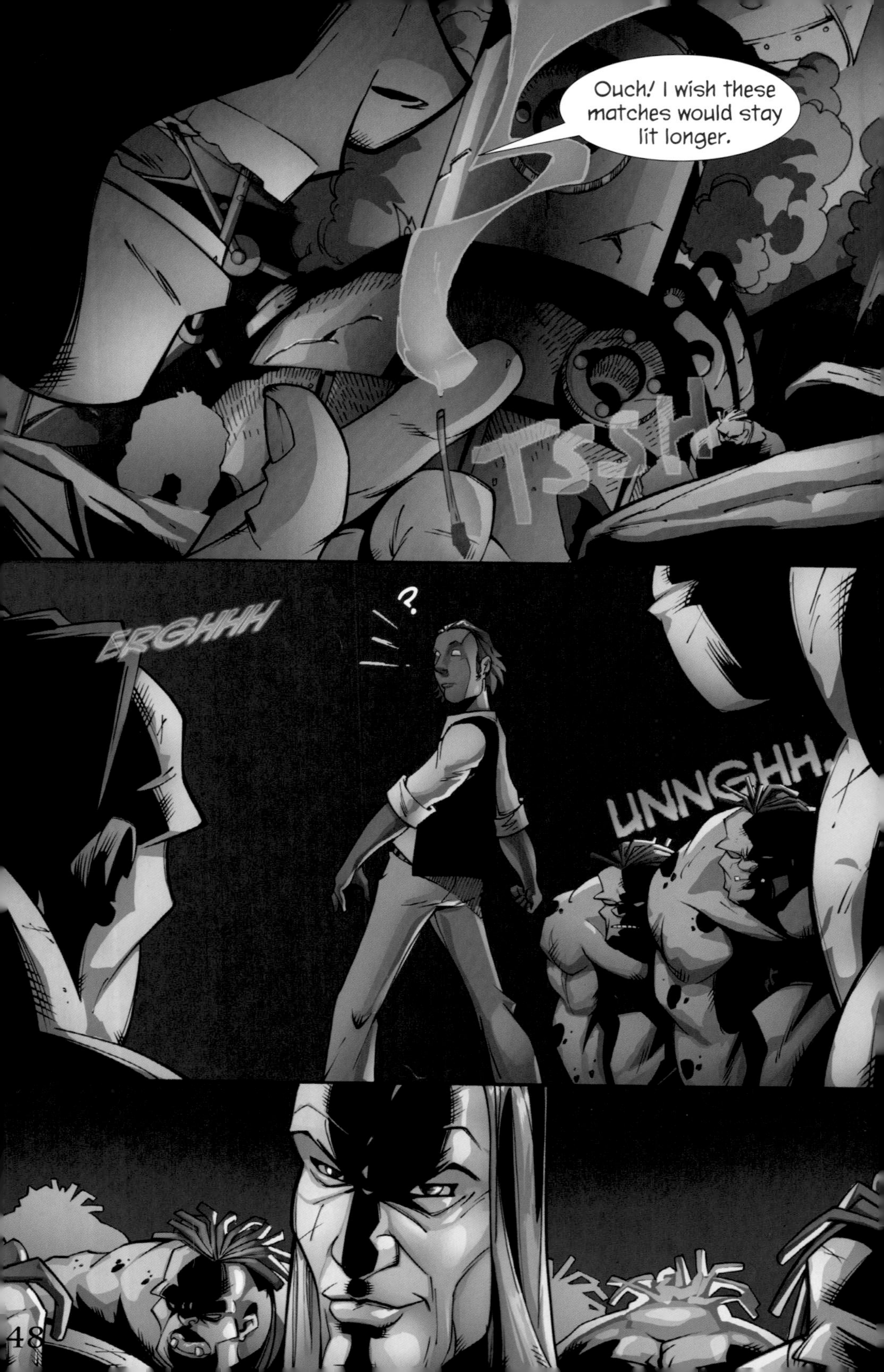
Ouch! I wish these matches would stay lit longer.
TSSH
ERGHHH
?
UNNGHH

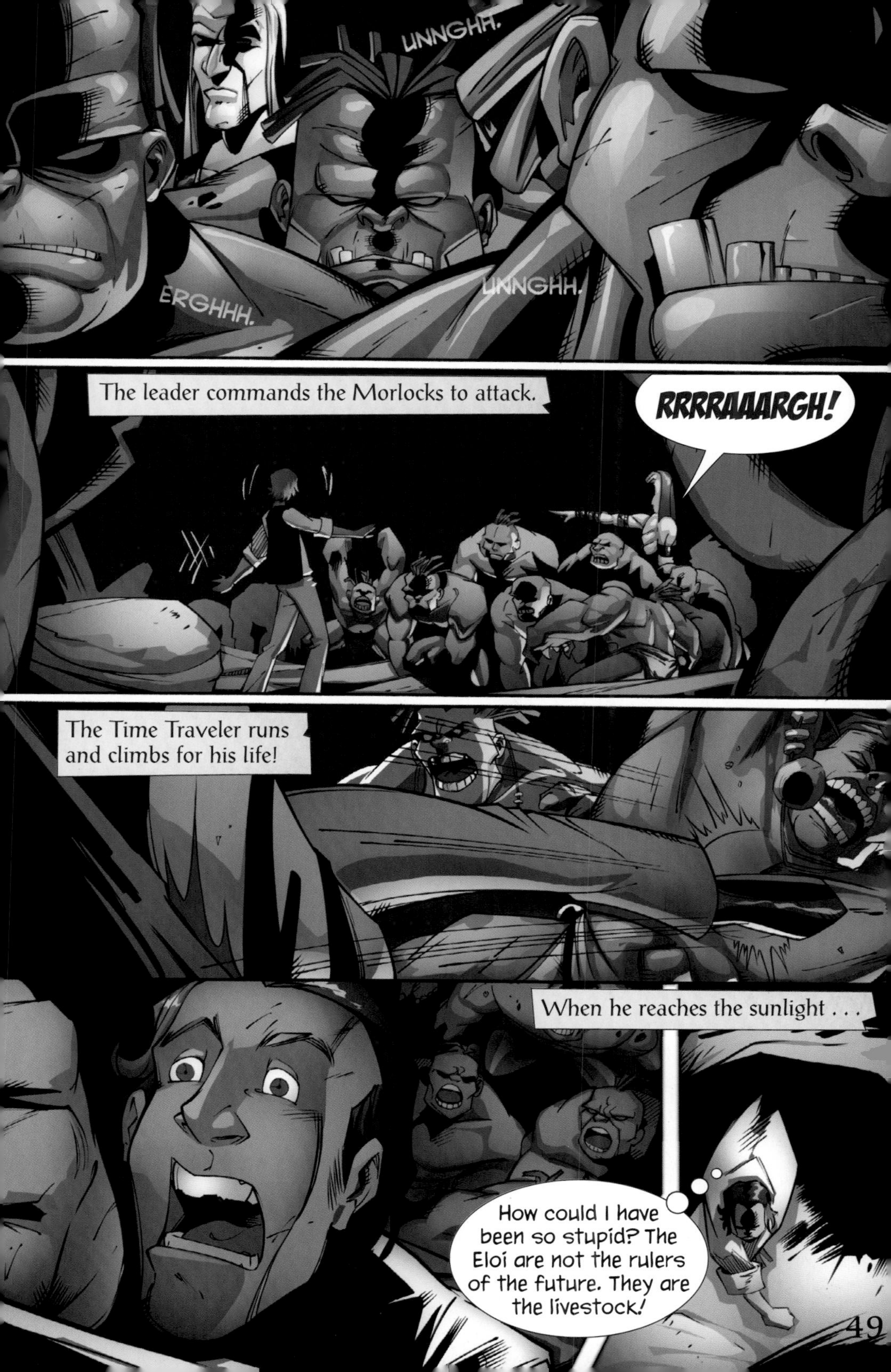
UNNGHH.
ERGHHH.
UNNGHH.
The leader commands the Morlocks to attack.
RRRRAAARGH!
The Time Traveler runs and climbs for his life!
When he reaches the sunlight . . .
How could I have been so stupid? The Eloi are not the rulers of the future. They are the livestock!

CHAPTER 6: The Forest Fire

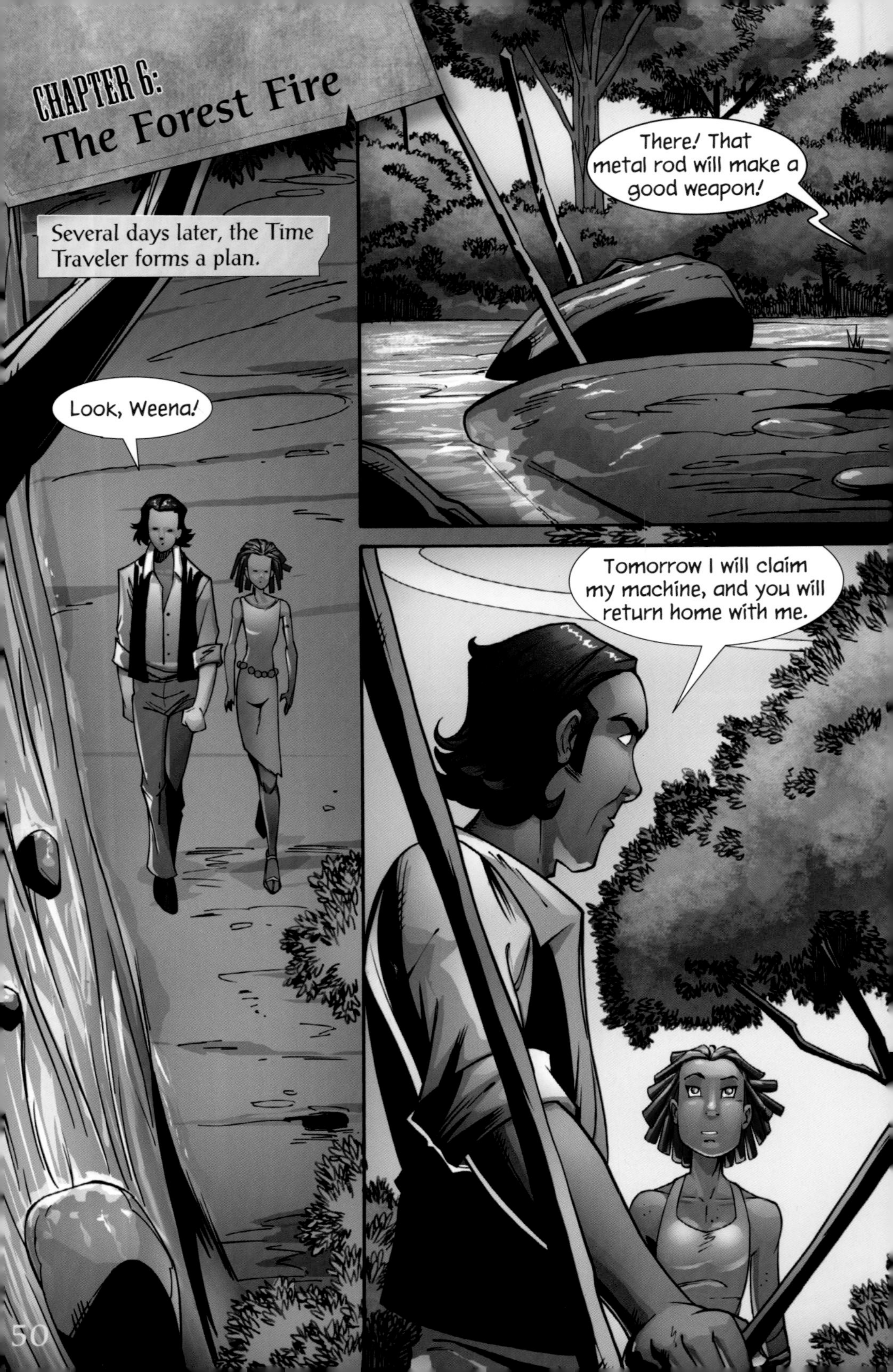
Several days later, the Time Traveler forms a plan.
Look, Weena!
There! That metal rod will make a good weapon!
Tomorrow I will claim my machine, and you will return home with me.

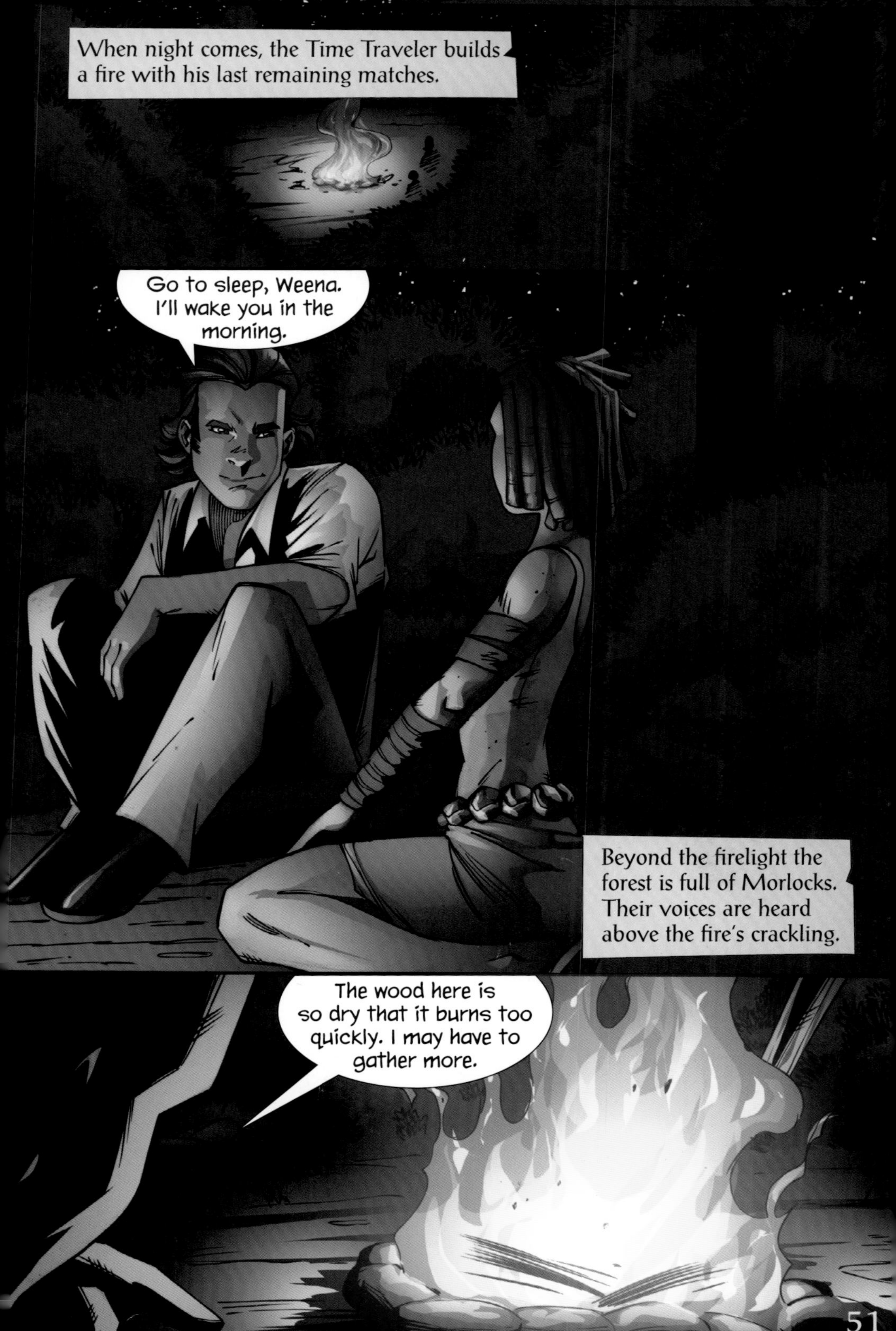

When night comes, the Time Traveler builds a fire with his last remaining matches.
Go to sleep, Weena. I'll wake you in the morning.
Beyond the firelight the forest is full of Morlocks. Their voices are heard above the fire's crackling.
The wood here is so dry that it burns too quickly. I may have to gather more.

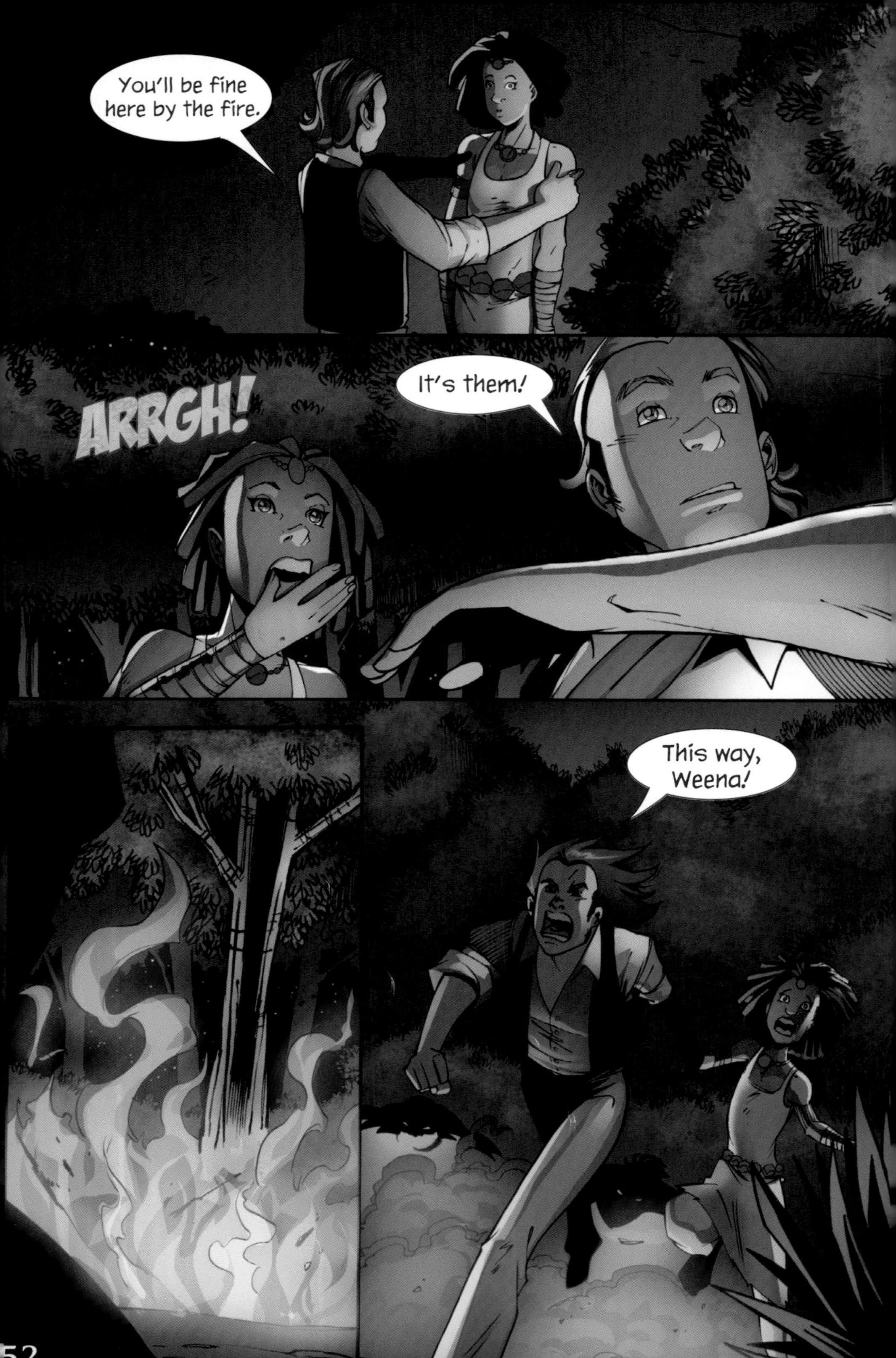
You'll be fine here by the fire.
ARRGH!
It's them!
This way, Weena!

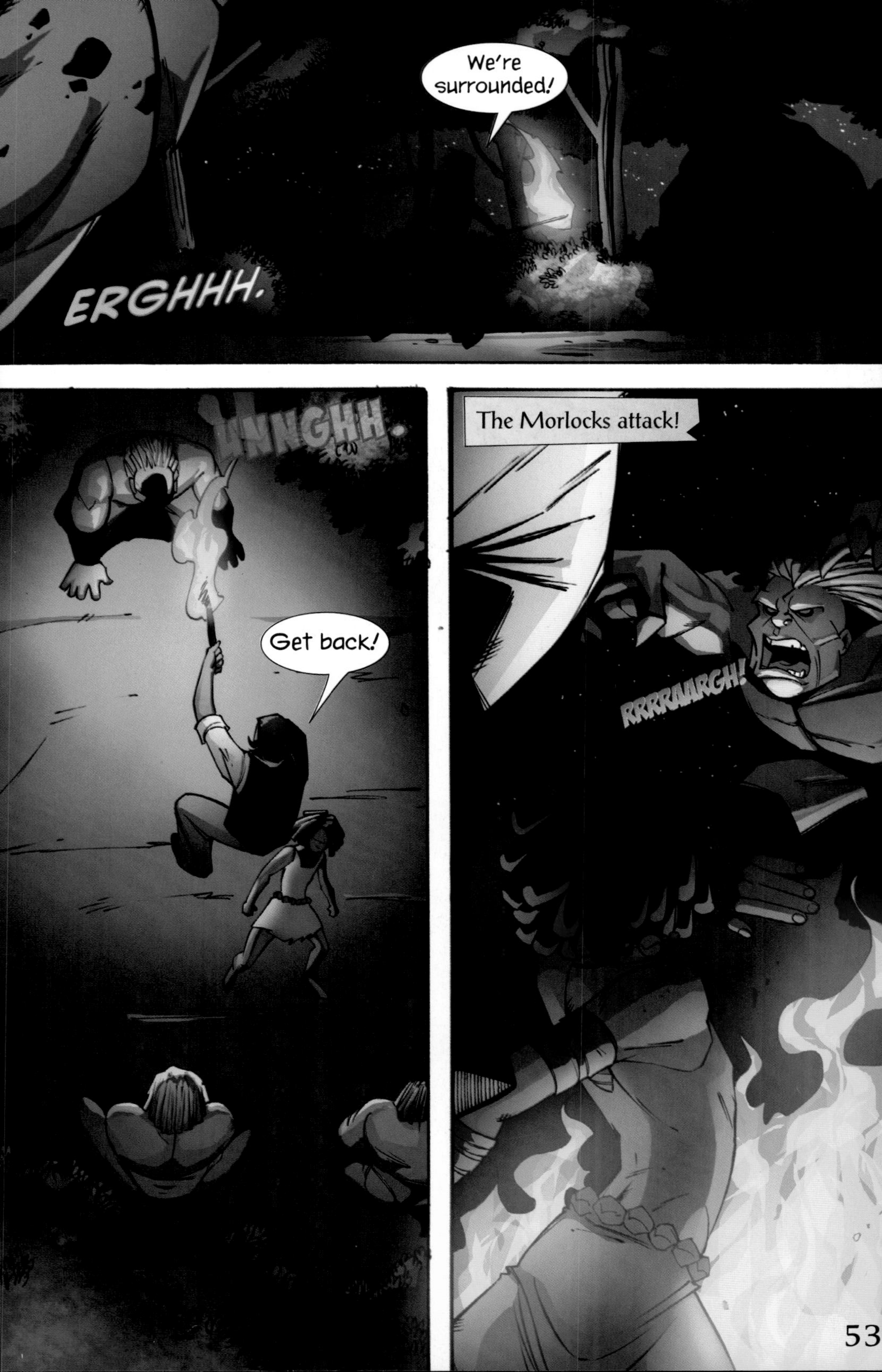

We're surrounded!
ERGHHH.
UNNGHH.
Get back!
The Morlocks attack!
RRRRAARGH!

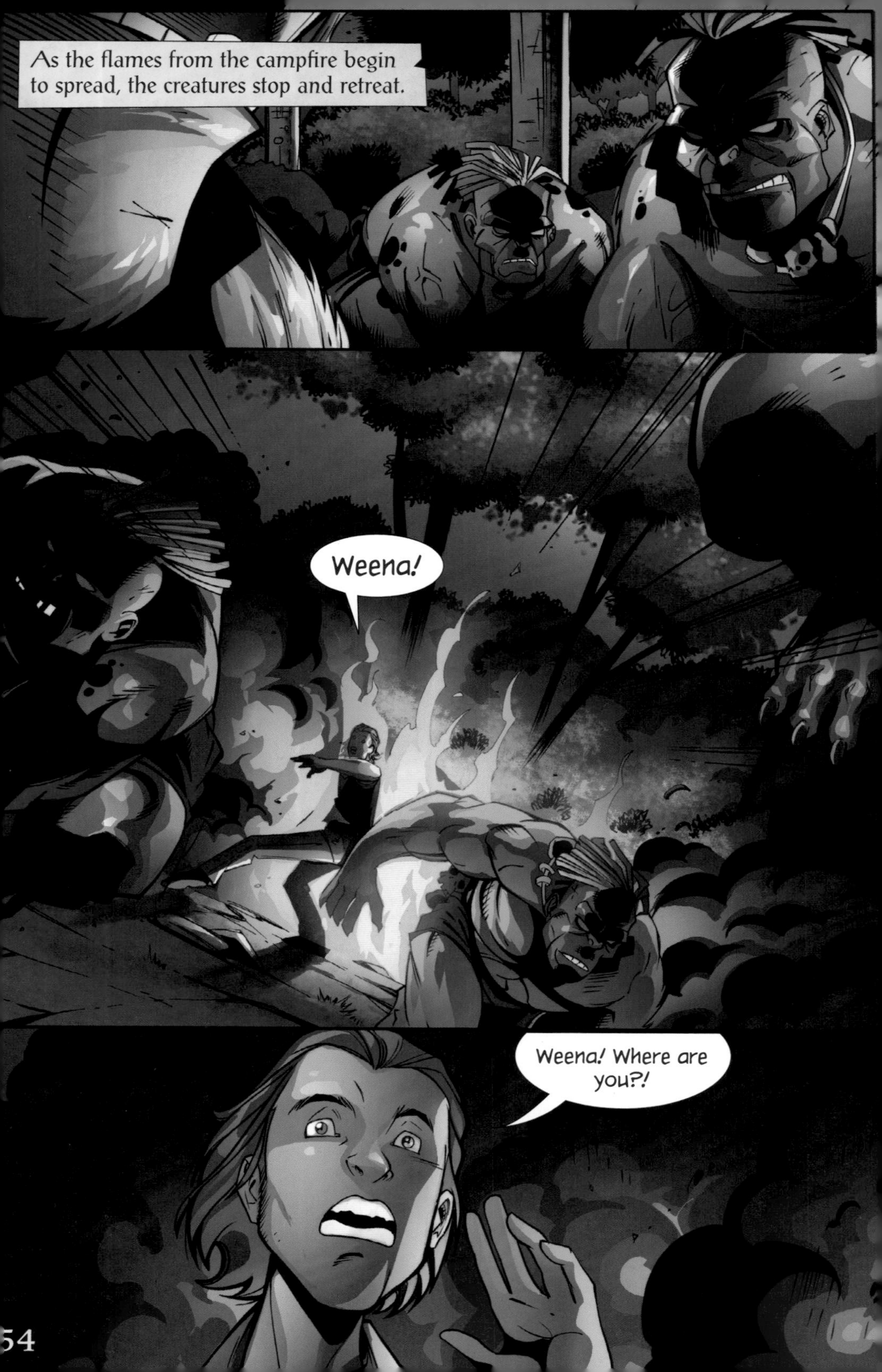
As the flames from the campfire begin to spread, the creatures stop and retreat.
Weena!
Weena! Where are you?!

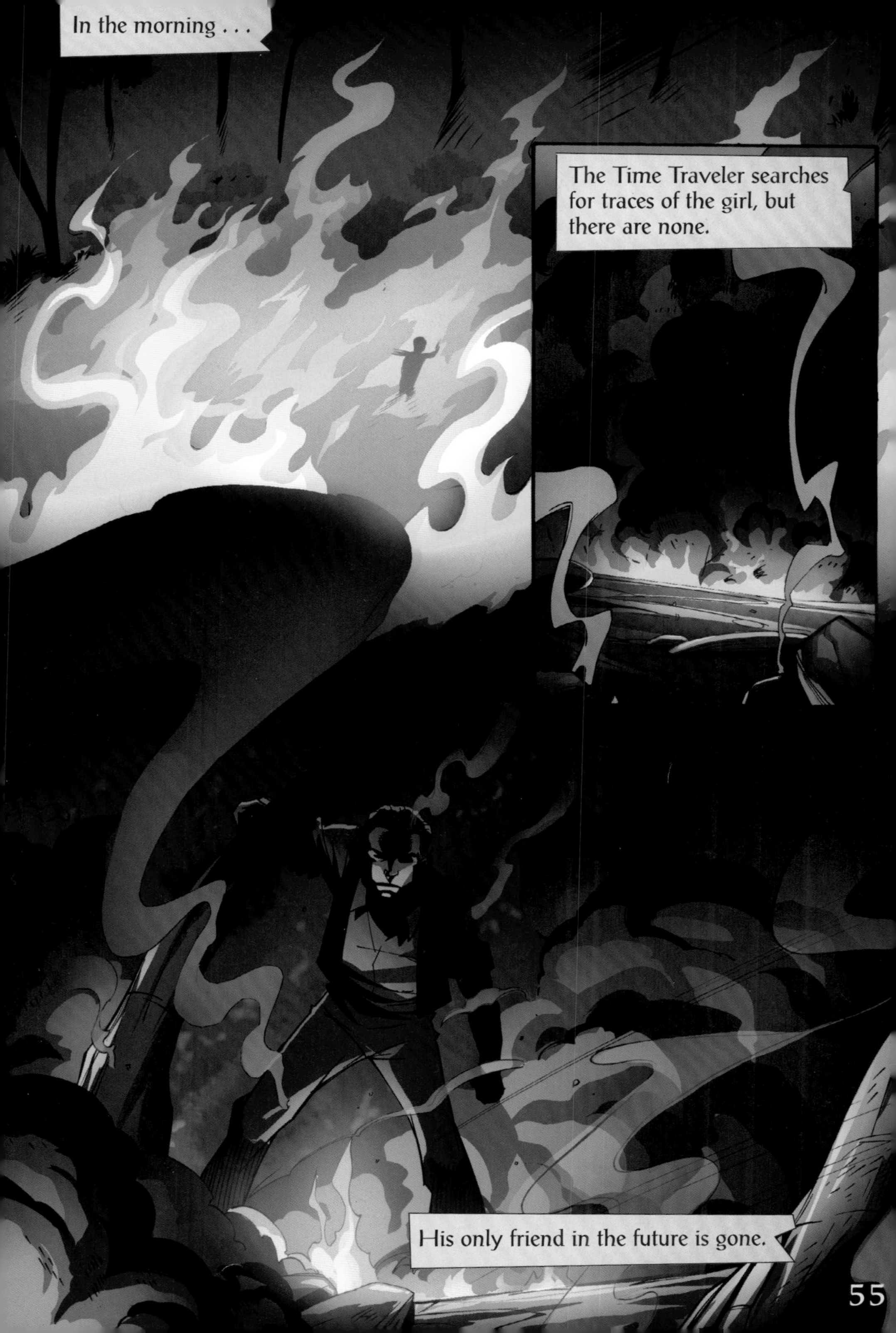
In the morning . . .
The Time Traveler searches for traces of the girl, but there are none.
His only friend in the future is gone.

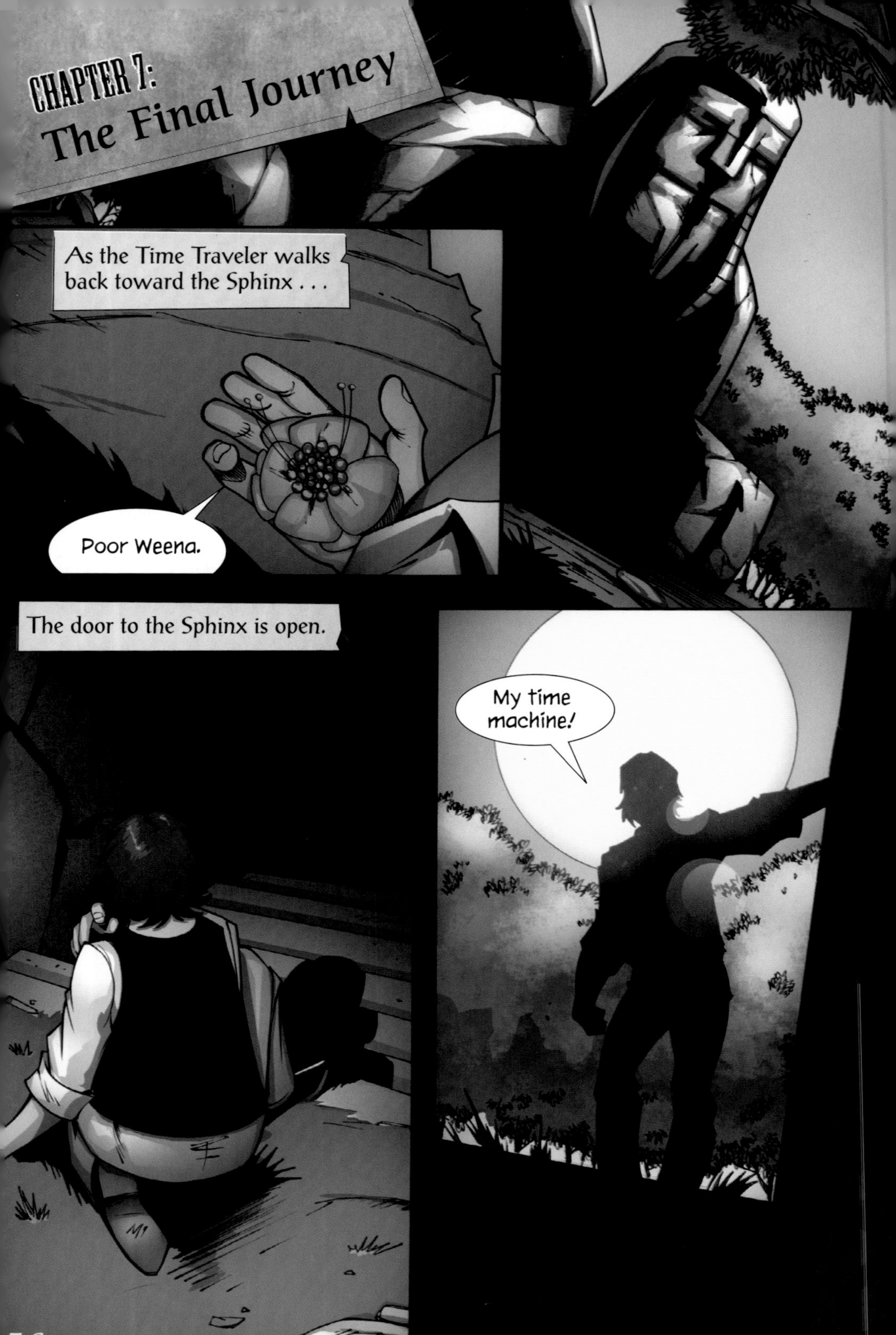

CHAPTER 7:
The Final Journey
As the Time Traveler walks back toward the Sphinx . . .
Poor Weena.
The door to the Sphinx is open.
My time machine!

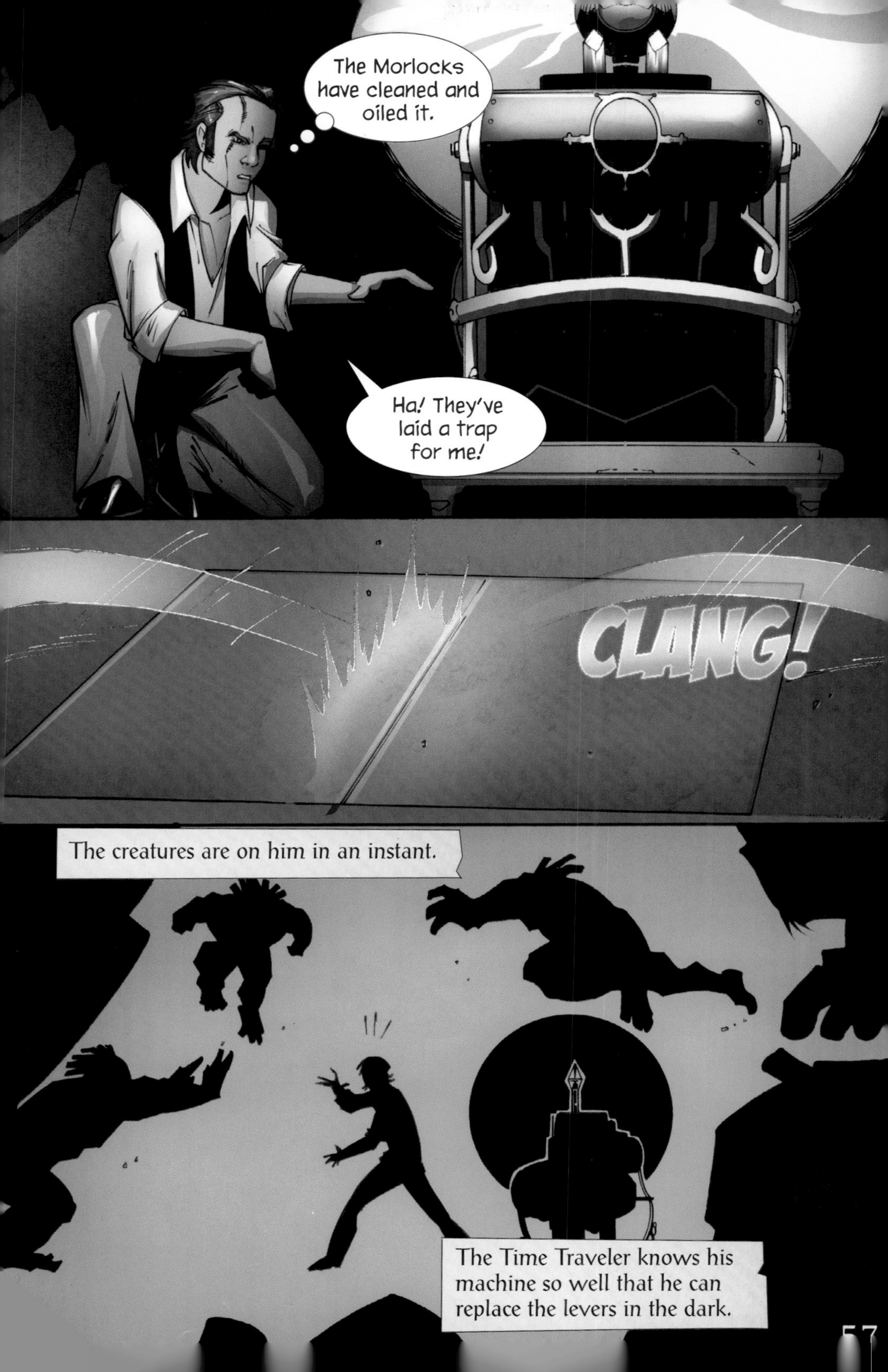
The Morlocks have cleaned and oiled it.
Ha! They've laid a trap for me!
CLANG!
The creatures are on him in an instant.
The Time Traveler knows his machine so well that he can replace the levers in the dark.

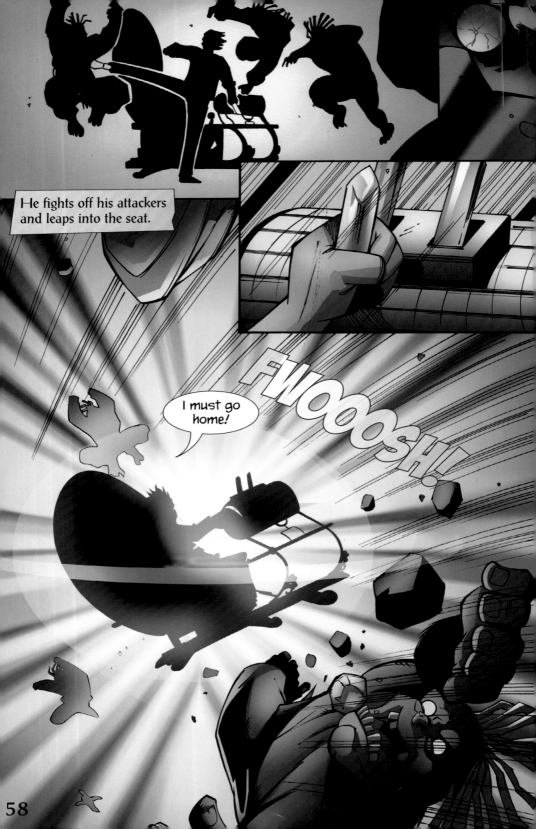

He fights off his attackers and leaps into the seat.

I must go home!

FWOOOSH!

58

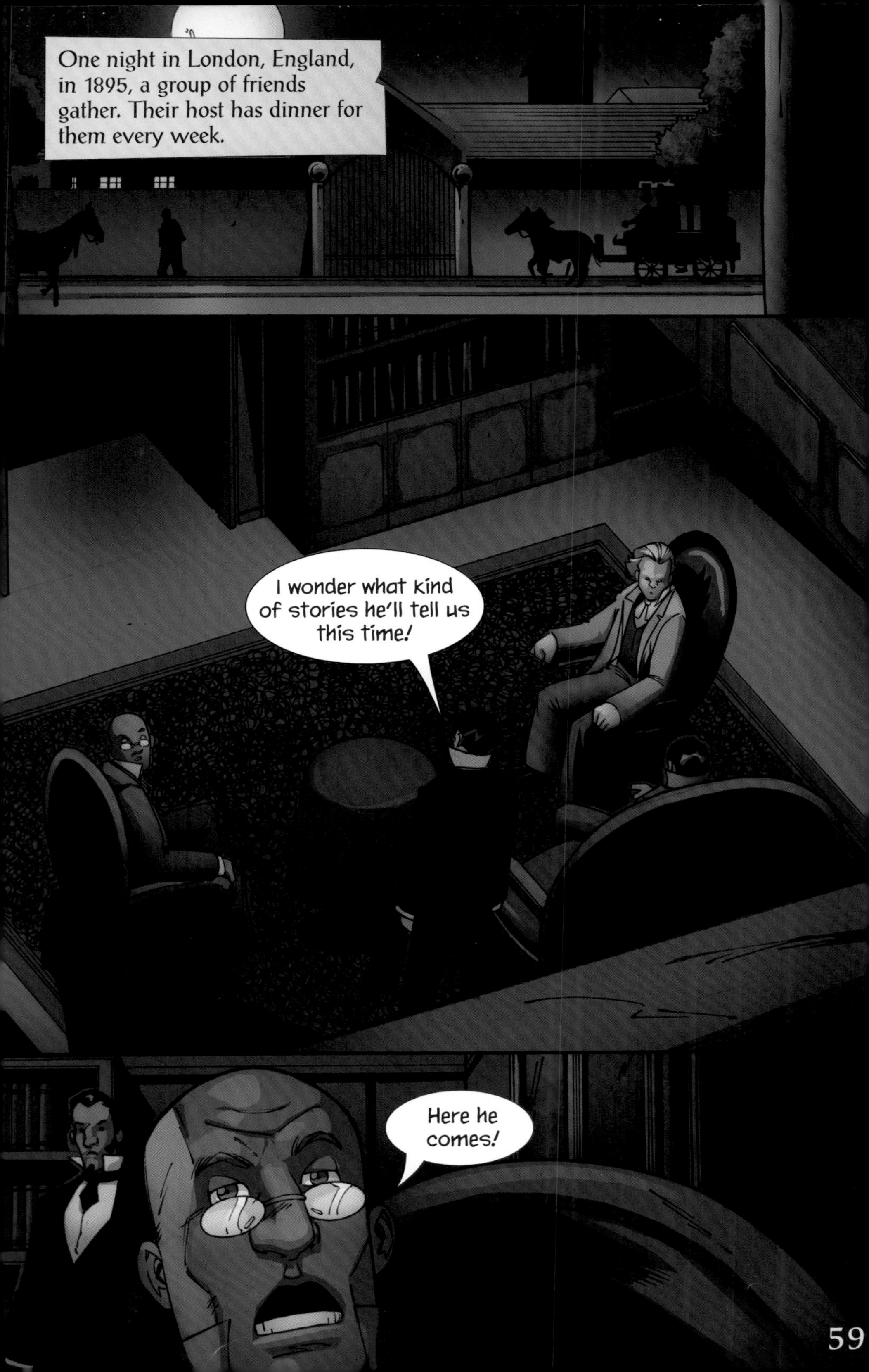
One night in London, England, in 1895, a group of friends gather. Their host has dinner for them every week.
I wonder what kind of stories he'll tell us this time!
Here he comes!

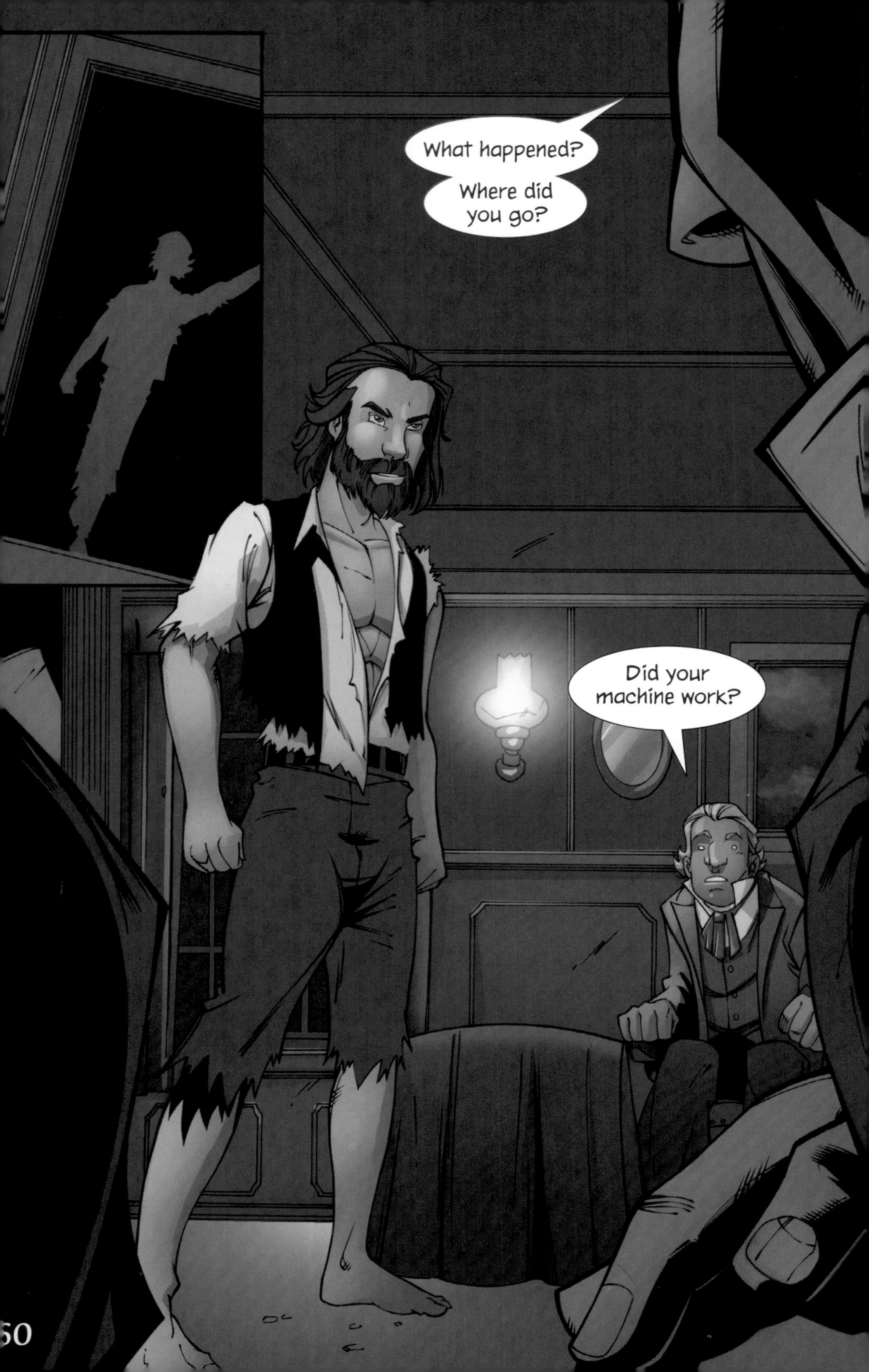
What happened?
Where did you go?
Did your machine work?

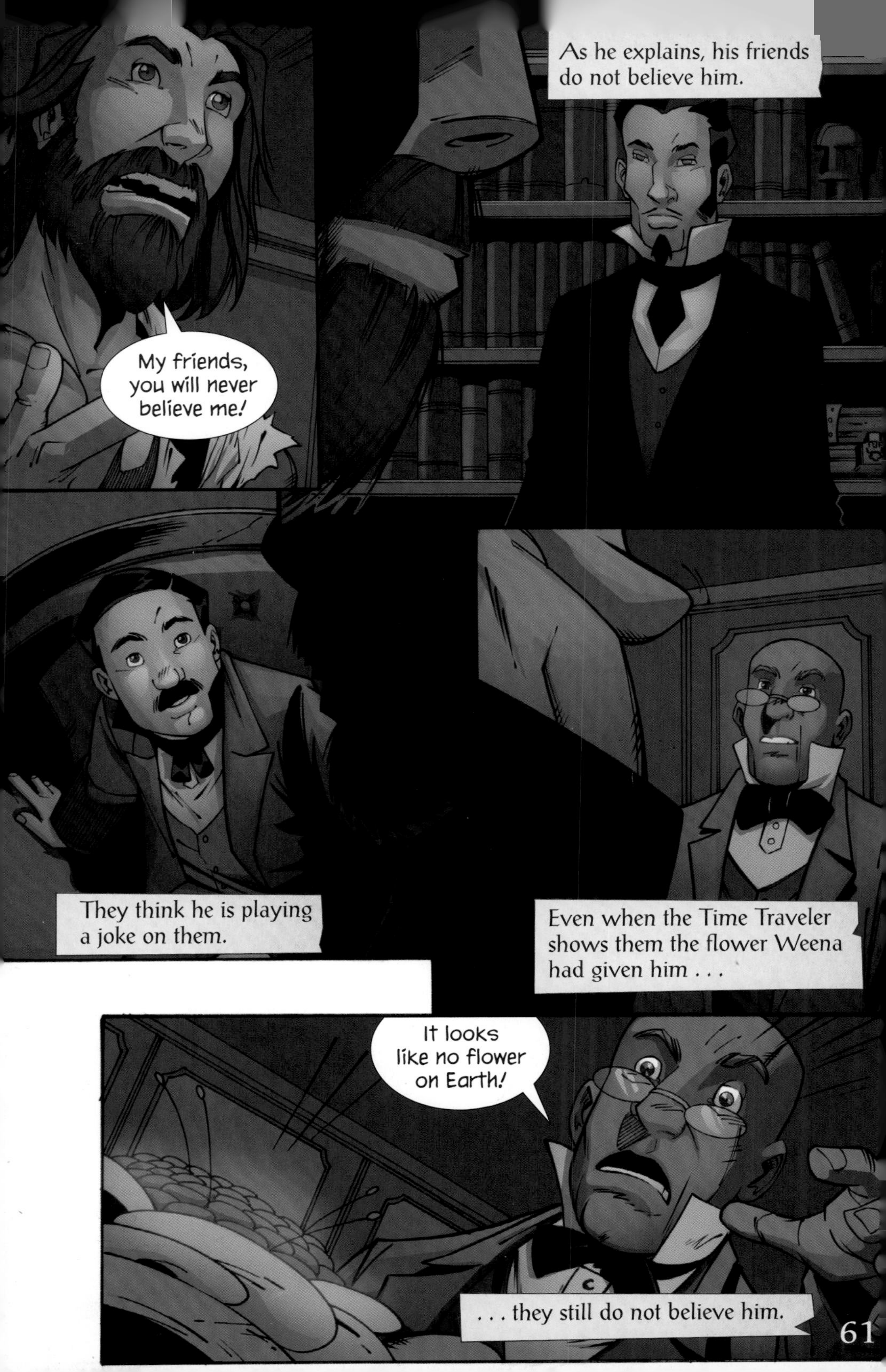

As he explains, his friends do not believe him.
My friends, you will never believe me!
They think he is playing a joke on them.
Even when the Time Traveler shows them the flower Weena had given him . . .
It looks like no flower on Earth!
. . . they still do not believe him.

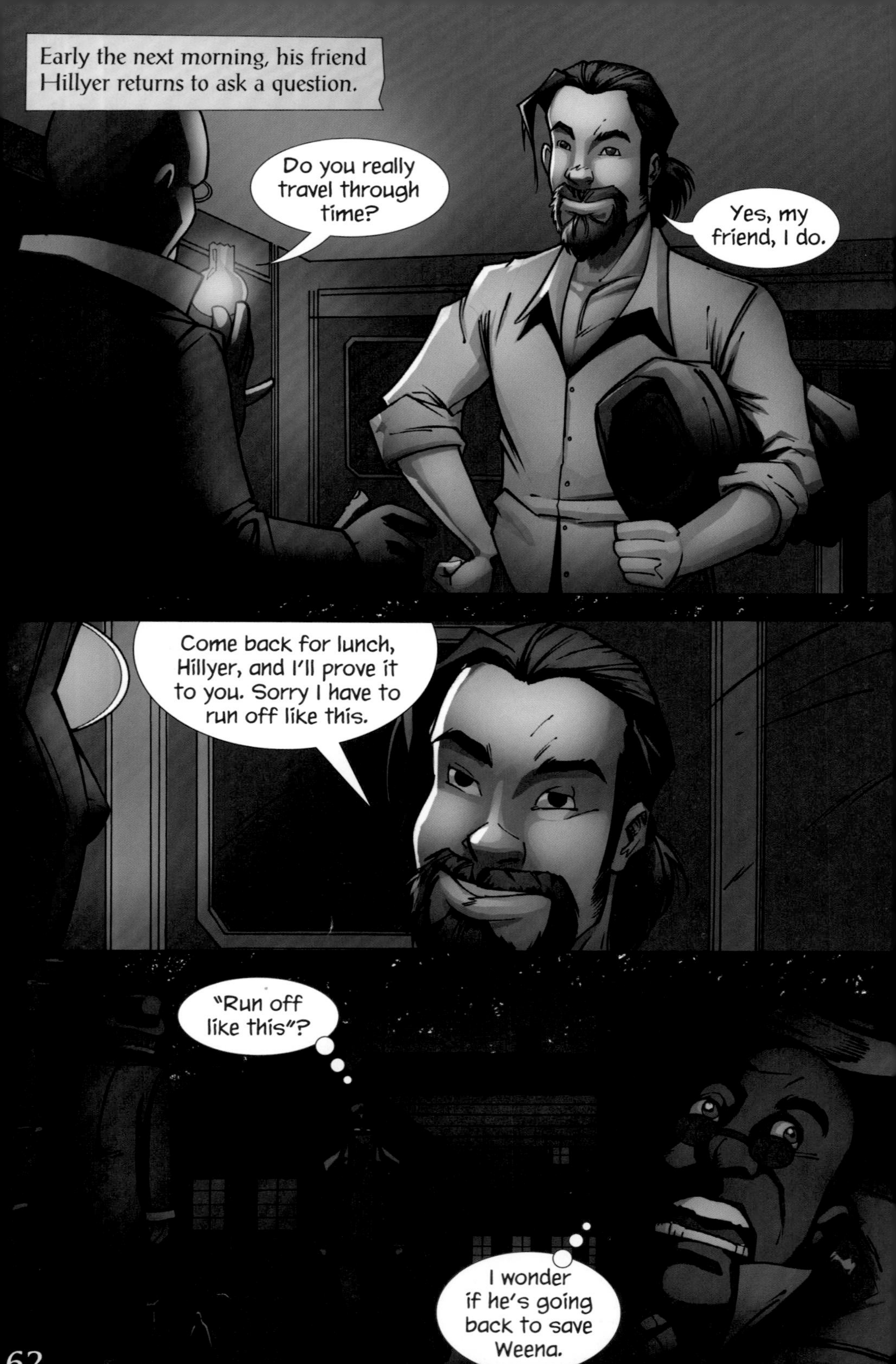

Early the next morning, his friend Hillyer returns to ask a question.
Do you really travel through time?
Yes, my friend, I do.
Come back for lunch, Hillyer, and I'll prove it to you. Sorry I have to run off like this.
"Run off like this"?
I wonder if he's going back to save Weena.

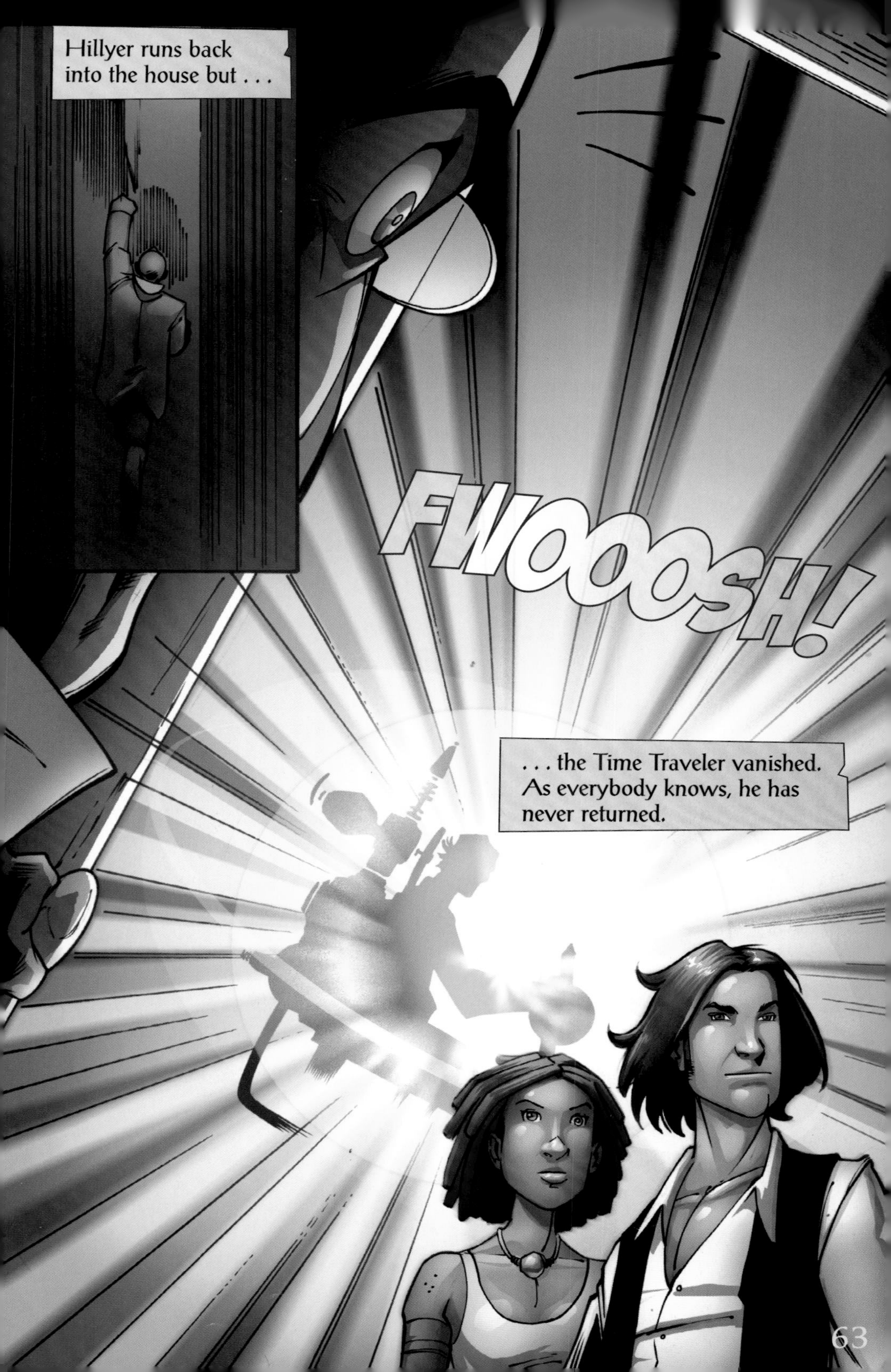
Hillyer runs back into the house but . . .
FWOOOSH!
. . . the Time Traveler vanished. As everybody knows, he has never returned.

ABOUT
H.G. WELLS

Herbert George Wells was born on September 21, 1866, in England. At age 7, he suffered a broken leg. While resting from his injury, Wells started reading books. As he grew older, he continued to enjoy reading and school. At 14, young Wells quit school to help his struggling family. Fortunately, he received a scholarship in 1883 and began studying science at a school in London. Soon after, Wells started writing. Some of his works, like *The Time Machine*, combine his love for storytelling and science.

ABOUT THE
RETELLING AUTHOR

As a teenager, Terry Davis was a third-string shooting guard for his junior varsity basketball team. In his junior year, Davis turned to wrestling. He took to the sport like a bear to a honeycomb and wrestled his remaining high school years. Today, Davis is a father, a writer, and — in his words — "a fat old wrestling coach." He also teaches narrative and screenwriting at Minnesota State University, Mankato.

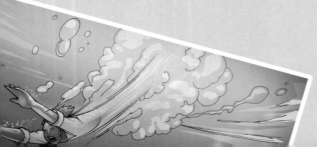

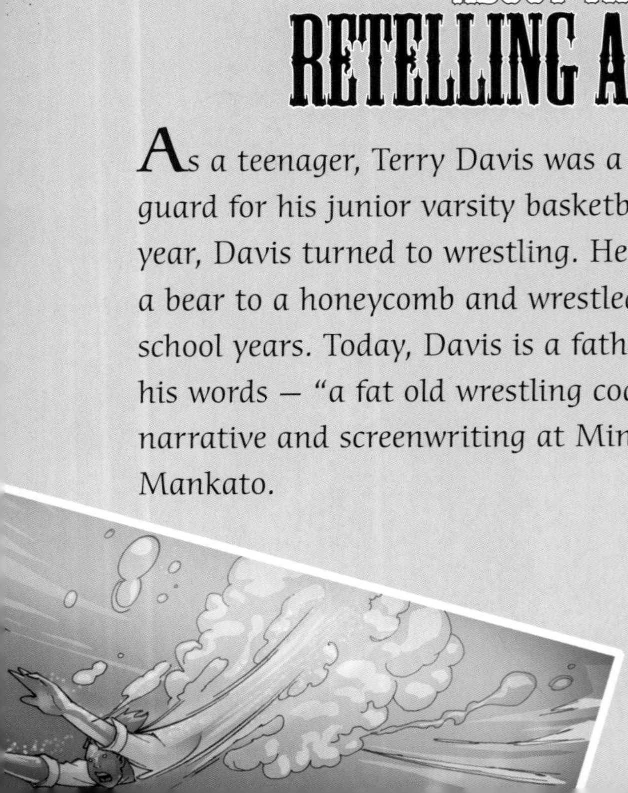

GLOSSARY

British Empire (BRIH-tish EM-pyr)—a former group of countries ruled by the British kings and queens

descend (di-SEND)—to climb down or go to a lower level

gauges (GAYG-ehz)—instruments used for measuring things such as time, pressure, or distance

glade (GLAYD)—an open, grassy space surrounded by woods

horseless carriage (HORSS-lehss KAIR-ij)—another name for an automobile; people called the first automobiles horseless carriages because they moved without being pulled by a horse.

livestock (LYV-stok)—animals raised on a farm, usually for food or to help with work; cows, sheep, and horses are all livestock.

Queen Victoria (KWEEN vik-TOR-ree-uh)—ruler of the British Empire from 1837 to 1901

Sphinx (SFINGKS)—a female monster in Greek mythology that has a woman's head, a lion's body, and wings

time machine (TYM muh-SHEEN)—a vehicle used to travel back to the past or into the future

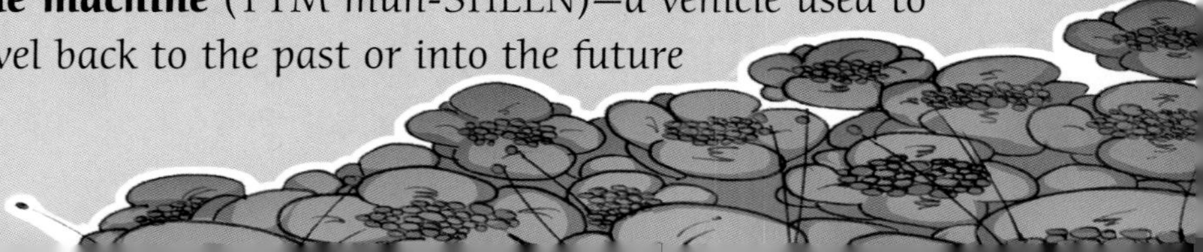

H. G. Wells imagined a very different world 800 centuries from now. So, what do scientists think the future will really be like? Here are a few of their predictions:

Scientists believe the Sun has already used up half of its energy. Luckily, this enormous ball of gas should keep burning for another 5 billion years!

In the story, the Time Traveler thinks the Sun seems closer and bigger. Scientists believe this could actually come true. As the Sun burns out, it will also grow and expand. Eventually, it could reach and absorb the earth.

Even before the Sun dies, the earth could get hotter. Scientists call the increasing temperatures global warming. Many believe that pollution could be clogging the air and trapping heat in the earth's atmosphere. By the year 2100, they think the earth could be 3.5 to 8 degrees warmer.

Will Morlocks and Eloi roam the earth in the future? Maybe not, but there will be plenty of people! Today, the total world population is about 6 billion. By the year 2050, scientists estimate a population of more than 9 billion.

Before any of these events happen, some scientists think humans will be living on other planets. In fact, in December 2006, the National Aeronautics and Space Administration (NASA) announced plans for a permanent base on the Moon. Starting in 2024, astronauts could live and work at the lunar base.

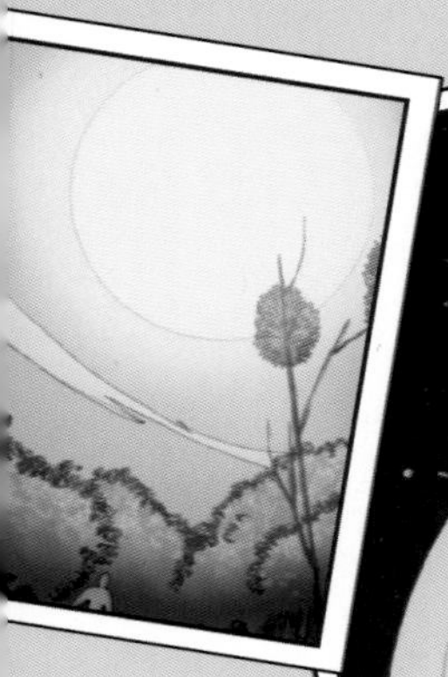

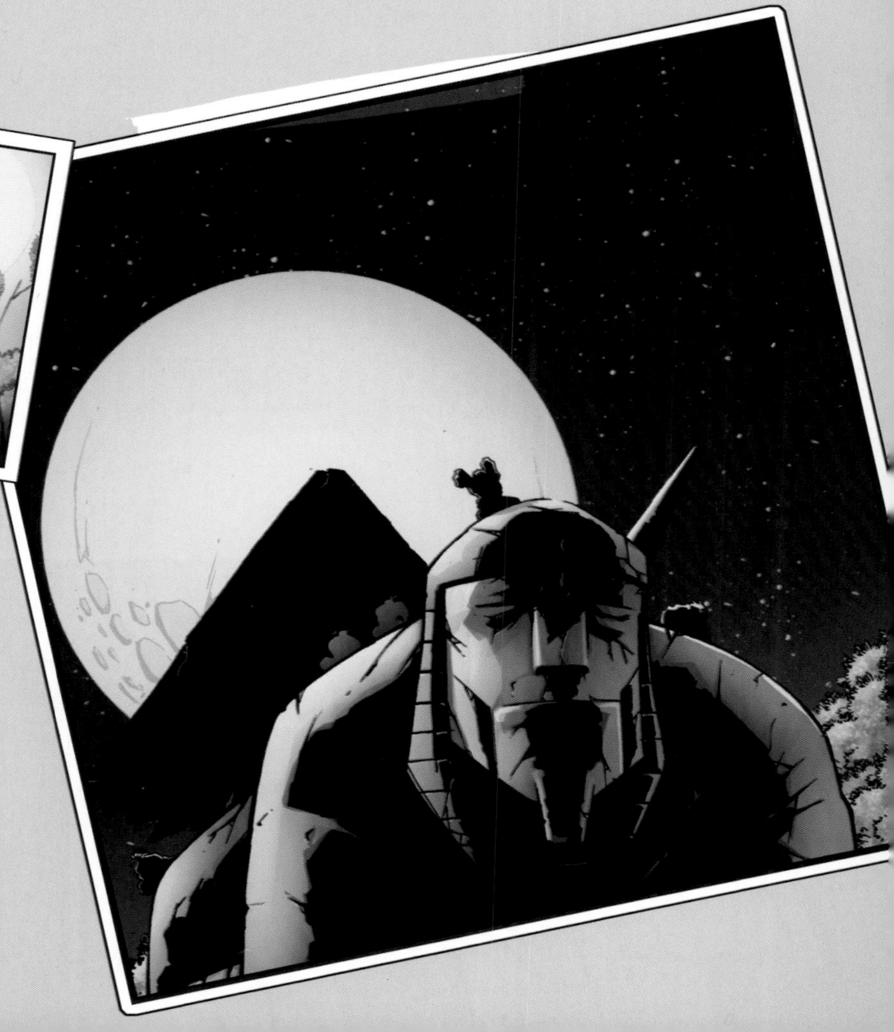

DISCUSSION QUESTIONS

1. The Time Traveler discovers that the world is a very different place in the year 8,027,011. Why do you think the world changed so much? Do you think the future is going to be like the author imagined?

2. What do you believe the Morlocks used their giant underground machine for?

3. While escaping from the Morlock tunnels, the Time Traveler realizes that the Eloi are the livestock of the future. What do you think the author means?

4. At the end of the story, Hillyer believes the Time Traveler went back to save Weena. Where do you think the Time Traveler went? Why?

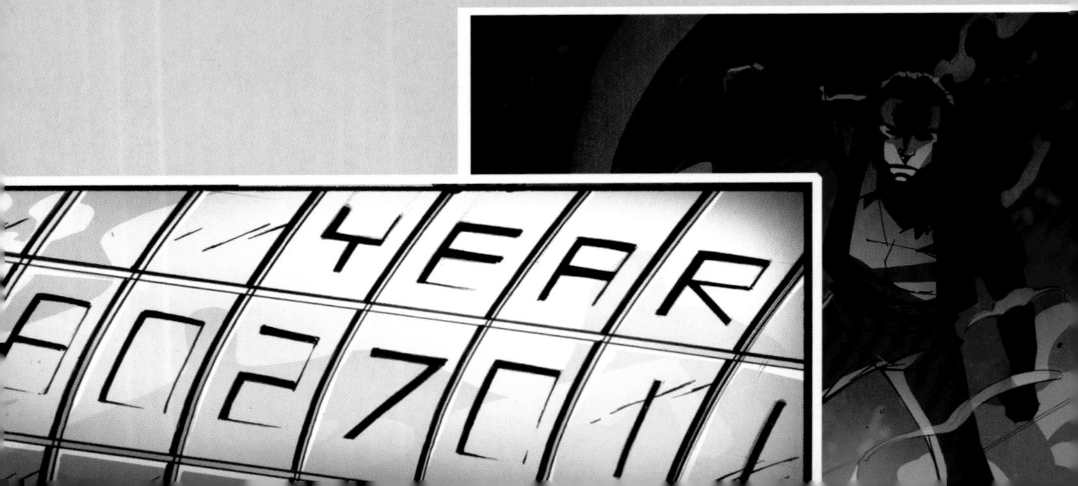
YEAR

WRITING PROMPTS

1. The Time Traveler took his time machine 800 centuries into the future. If you had a time machine would you travel to the future or the past? Describe where you would go and what you would find there.

2. The Time Traveler's friends don't believe that the time machine works. Describe a moment when someone didn't believe you. Why did they think you were lying?

3. At the end of the story, the Time Traveler vanishes. Where did he go? Was he reunited with Weena? How did the Time Traveler live the rest of his life? Write a new ending to the story that answers these questions.

OTHER BOOKS

THE INVISIBLE MAN
GRAPHIC NOVEL
by H. G. Wells
retold by
Terry Davis
illustrated by
Dennis Calero
STONE ARCH Classic Fiction

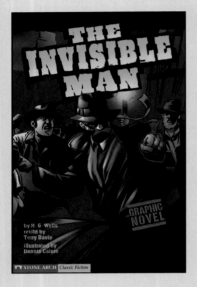

THE INVISIBLE MAN

Late one night, a mysterious man wanders into a tiny English village. He is covered from head to toe in bandages. After a series of burglaries, the villagers grow suspicious. Who is this man? Where did he come from? When the villagers attempt to arrest the stranger, he suddenly reveals his secret — he is invisible! How can anyone stop the Invisible Man?

JULES VERNE'S
JOURNEY TO THE CENTER OF THE EARTH
GRAPHIC NOVEL
STONE ARCH Classic Fiction

JOURNEY TO THE CENTER OF THE EARTH

Axel Lidenbrock and his uncle find a mysterious message inside a 300-year-old book. The dusty note describes a secret passageway to the center of the earth! Soon they are descending deeper and deeper into the heart of a volcano. With their guide Hans, the men discover underground rivers, oceans, strange rock formations, and prehistoric monsters. They also run into danger, which threatens to trap them below the surface forever.

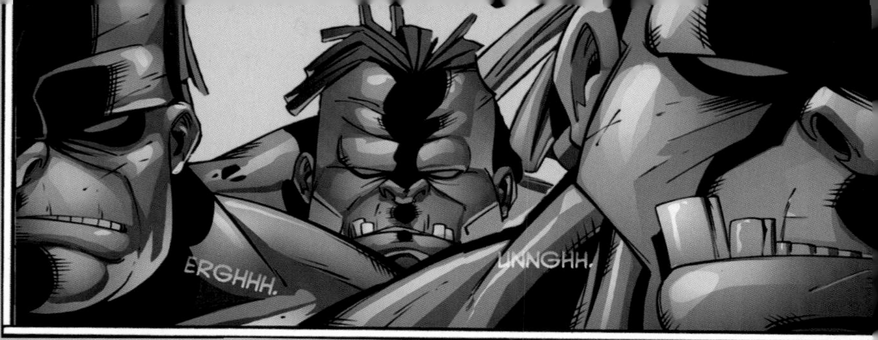
ERGHHH.
UNNGHH.

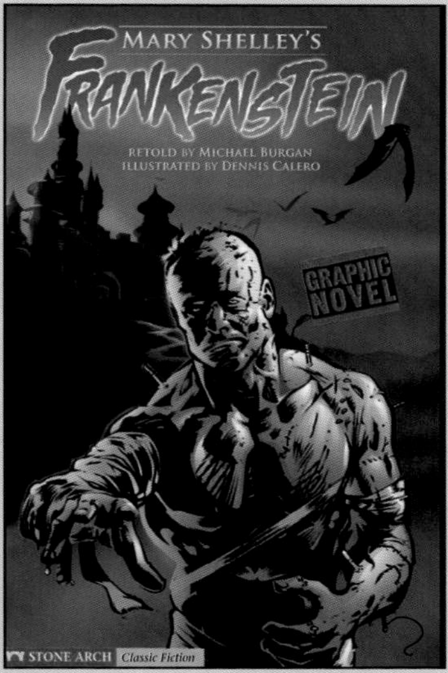
MARY SHELLEY'S
FRANKENSTEIN
RETOLD BY MICHAEL BURGAN
ILLUSTRATED BY DENNIS CALERO
GRAPHIC NOVEL
STONE ARCH Classic Fiction

FRANKENSTEIN

The young scientist Victor Frankenstein has created something amazing and horrible at the same time — a living being out of dead flesh and bone. His creation, however, turns out to be a monster! Frankenstein's creation quickly discovers that his hideous appearance frightens away any companions. Now Victor Frankenstein must stop his creation before the monster's loneliness turns to violence.

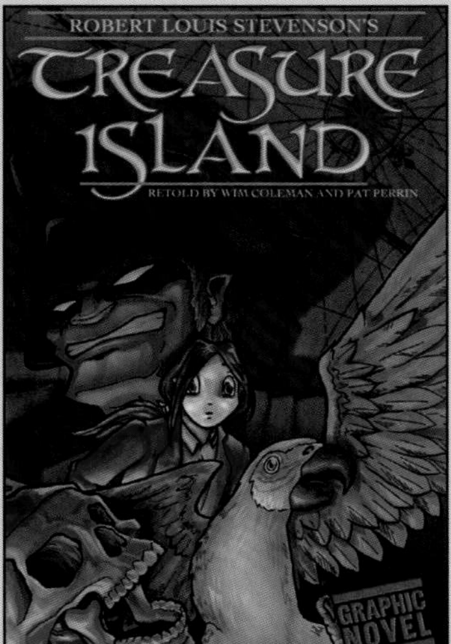
ROBERT LOUIS STEVENSON'S
TREASURE ISLAND
RETOLD BY WIM COLEMAN AND PAT PERRIN
GRAPHIC NOVEL
STONE ARCH Classic Fiction

TREASURE ISLAND

Jim Hawkins had no idea what he was getting into when the pirate Billy Bones showed up at the doorstep of his mother's inn. When Billy dies suddenly, Jim is left to unlock his old sea chest, which reveals money, a journal, and a treasure map. Joined by a band of honorable men, Jim sets sail on a dangerous voyage to locate the loot on a faraway island. The violent sea is only one of the dangers they face. They soon encounter a band of bloodthirsty pirates determined to make the treasure their own!

INTERNET SITES

Do you want to know more about subjects related to this book? Or are you interested in learning about other topics? Then check out FactHound, a fun, easy way to find Internet sites.

Our investigative staff has already sniffed out great sites for you!

Here's how to use FactHound:

1. Visit *www.facthound.com*

2. Select your grade level.

3. To learn more about subjects related to this book, type in the book's ISBN number: **1598898337**.

4. Click the **Fetch It** button.

FactHound will fetch the best Internet sites for you!